A
HARLEQUIN
Book

A CHANCE TO WIN

Original title: *The Lottery for Matthew Devlin*

by

MARGARET ROME

HARLEQUIN BOOKS

Winnipeg • Canada   New York • New York

A CHANCE TO WIN

First published in 1968 by Mills & Boon Limited,
50 Grafton Way, Fitzroy Square, London, England,
under the title *The Lottery for Matthew Devlin*.

Harlequin Canadian edition published June, 1969
Harlequin U.S. edition published September, 1969

Standard Book Number: 373-51307-0.

CHAPTER I

'WHY, the man's an absolute beast!'

Liz Doran lifted an interrogatory eyebrow and twisted round from her indolent position on the couch where she lay to inquire of her usually serene and composed flat-mate, Nicola Brent:

'Who's a beast, darling? Can I meet him? I adore beastly men!'

Nicola looked up from the letter she was reading through for a second time in case she had misunderstood its message after her first swift appraisal of it and lifted stormy green eyes in her friend's direction. She looked as if she would give her flippant remark a sharp answer, but when Liz threw up her arms in mock terror and pretended to cower from the wrath to come she laughed unwillingly and the sparks fled from her eyes to be replaced by a look of smouldering resentment.

'This letter,' she waved it in front of Liz's slightly *retroussé* nose, 'is from my Aunt Sarah. She tells me that Matthew Devlin has actually had the audacity to dismiss my cousin Dulcie at a moment's notice and has refused to give her a reference. How dare he!' Her voice rose with indignation as she went on, stressing her contempt of the man with each syllable. 'She has no idea why she was dismissed and refuses even to discuss it with her mother. Aunt Sarah says Dulcie came home from work two days ago terribly upset, told her the bare fact of her dismissal, and then rushed up to her room and stayed there for hours crying bitterly. Aunt Sarah managed to coax her downstairs for a bite to eat when she was more composed, but she absolutely refuses to tell her mother another thing. She says she just wants to forget about it. Forget about it, indeed! Forget the four years she's slaved as that horrible man's secretary just to be cast off like an old hat when it suits him!'

All her inbred dislike of the owners of Scaur Bank Mills was evident in her tone as she bit off the name of her cousin Dulcie's ex-employer.

'Matt Devlin! Son of a rake and a true son of his father. I hate him! Hate them both!'

Liz stared with open-mouthed amazement at Nicola's flushed, mutinous face and clenched fists. In all of the five years she had known her—and in the latter two of the five years since they had shared the flat which they were now occupying they had become very firm friends— she had had no indication of the depth of feeling of which her friend was capable.

Nicola Brent was private secretary to the director of the model agency where she, Liz, had been employed until she had decided to go freelance, and was the hub around which the whole of the agency revolved. Nicola had never been known to get flustered. Her calm, sensible presence could guarantee to soothe the jagged nerves of highly temperamental models and artists, and her swift, competent assessment of a situation never failed to bring satisfied smiles to the faces of individuals who, moments before her intervention, would have been threatening hysterics. And now here she was, showing herself capable of more temper and downright anger than any of her most difficult clients.

Liz gazed at her admiringly, and when she had found her voice, gasped, 'Darling, you should lose your temper more often; it does things for you! You look absolutely fabulous when your big green eyes are emitting sparks, and that red hair of yours is crackling; I swear it is!'

Nicola looked at her in despair and then threw herself

into a large chubby armchair opposite and began to laugh ruefully.

'Liz, can't you ever be serious? Must you see everything from a model's point of view? This man must be taught a lesson. He mustn't be allowed to get away with his high-handedness! I shall have to think of some way of helping Dulcie. Be a love and get the supper while I try to sort out my thoughts, will you?'

Liz acquiesced gracefully and unwound her long legs, clad in black velvet tights, from under her. She was taller than Nicola and her smooth black tresses contrasted vividly with Nicola's auburn hair. The two girls were utterly dissimilar in looks and nature, for while Nicola was, as a rule, of a very calm, madonna-like temperament, Liz, although physically inclined to be lazy, was of a volatile and excitable nature and had a penchant for gathering scores of young admirers round her; in direct opposition to Nicola, whose unwittingly 'touch me not' aura gave rise to a feeling of hesitancy and uncertainty in the hearts of her would-be admirers. Liz, whose life was not completed until she had a fresh admirer on her horizon, often berated her for her lack of interest in men in general, but nothing that she said could make any impression upon her friend. She simply wasn't interested.

Liz's face, as she prepared their supper, was troubled. Nicola's impulsive loyalty to her aunt and her cousin Dulcie was a typical reaction of a girl who felt the need to repay, in any way she could, the people who had been good enough to take her, when a bewildered eight-year-old orphan, and welcome her into their own family. Not that they were complete strangers, for Nicola's mother and Richard Dawson had been brother and sister and when her parents had both been killed in a car accident Nicola's only other living relative had been her Uncle Richard. He hadn't hesitated to take the shivering, lonely little mite, numbed with the shock of losing the core of her little world in one fell swoop, and to tell her, not without misgiving as he thought about what Sarah, his wife, would have to say when he presented Nicola as a permanent member of their household: 'You're not to weep any more, Nicola, do you hear me? From now on you will be part of my family; a sister for baby Dulcie. Will you like that, do you think? You'll be able to play with her and you'll sleep together and be great friends. I know she's only four years old, but she'll soon be a companion for you, and you'll learn to love her, and she you.'

Trustingly, she had put her hand in his, and from that day, and up to the day eight years later when he too had died, he had been her idol, comforter and, unknown to Nicola, her shield from the sharp tongue of her Aunt Sarah, whose resentment of her sister-in-law's child had been hard to mask.

Early in their acquaintance Nicola had told Liz of the kindness she had received from her uncle and his family and of how, when Richard had died, her Aunt Sarah had made all the arrangements for Nicola to come to London and to get the job which had enabled her to begin to pay back her aunt some of the money that had been spent on her education.

Willingly, she had consented to put up at a hostel until she had time to look round for a more permanent place to live, and from her very first pay packet she had sent a small amount of money to begin to pay back her debt to her aunt. As her salary had grown so had her contributions to the family expenses, and although she must, by now, have paid for her commercial training a hundred times over, she still continued to pay unstintingly.

'She's nothing but an old Scrooge!' muttered Liz to herself as she banged the cups on the tray, ready to take it into the lounge where they usually had their supper, 'but it would be useless to say anything to Nicola about her. She's absolutely blind to her faults. And to Dulcie's!'

Liz rather prided herself on being a good judge of character, and after having been persuaded by Nicola to spend a weekend with her at her aunt's, she had been very disagreeably surprised to meet, not the sweet-tempered, generous-natured lover of orphans she had envisaged from Nicola's eulogies, but a petty, ill-tempered woman with the tight screwed-up mouth of a perpetual nag and the whining voice of a chronic moaner.

Her daughter, too, had struck Liz unfavourably on that seemingly endless weekend, for, whatever she had been used to doing when Nicola was not there to help out with the chores, on that particular weekend she had taken herself off at every available opportunity and left Nicola and Liz with the lot. Far from being a respite for the two girls it had turned out to be a lazy two days for both Sarah and Dulcie, and Liz could have kicked Nicola for her obtuseness, as far as they were concerned, when she had said to Liz :

'Poor dears! They really should have some permanent help in the house. Aunt Sarah says she's positively exhausted, and I don't wonder at it, she gives too much of herself in helping others!'

Liz clenched her teeth even now at the thought of how easily taken in Nicola was by what she termed to herself 'those two parasites'.

She cleared the frown from her face and walked into the lounge with their supper-tray.

Nicola turned to her with a grateful smile. 'Oh, Liz, you are a love. I'm just dying for a cuppa!'

Liz put the tray down in front of her and poured the amber-coloured liquid into the two fine china cups that were their pride and joy. They had found them in an old antique shop on one of their frequent flat-furnishing forages and had decided that, although there were only two cups and saucers and plates, they would have them for their own personal use and bring out the Woolworth china for their guests.

As they sat taking luxurious sips from the dainty fluted cups Liz waited expectantly for her friend's confidences. She was not disappointed but was decidedly dismayed when, finally, Nicola told her :

'It's not a bit of good, Liz. I'll have to go home and see for myself what's going on. Perhaps Dulcie will talk to me about it. In any case, I can't leave Aunt Sarah to worry alone, I must go and see what I can do.'

'But, Nicola, what about your job? You know how lost they'll be without you !'

'I'm due a week's holiday, I'll take that. I probably won't be away for the whole of the week, so if they're pushed I'll go to the office and help them out as soon as I get back. Then I can have a couple of days later on when we're not so busy.'

'I can just picture Mr. Harding's face when you go in and tell him that you want a week's holiday at a moment's notice,' said Liz dryly, 'and at the busiest time of the year, too. He'll be confounded.'

Nicola looked troubled, but compressed her firm young lips determinedly and said : 'I can't help that. After all,' she went on, 'I've delayed taking my holidays to help him out because we've been so busy. If I put it off any longer he'll take it for granted that I'm willing to forgo it. I know what he is, in that respect. He makes sure that he gets his holidays when he wants them, but is quite willing to overlook mine if it suits him to do so. He's a good boss, as you know, Liz, but like all men he puts himself first. Well, this time he'll have to put up with a secretary from the agency if the work piles up while I'm away. Aunt Sarah and Dulcie must come first. I owe it to them to help all I can.'

Liz shrugged resignedly. She knew that once having made up her mind Nicola would not budge. To all intents and purposes she was already on the train that would take her to Carswell, the old walled city that straddled the border between England and Scotland, where she had been raised as a child and which housed the infamous Matt Devlin, owner of Scaur Bank Mills and the cause of all the contention.

Liz gave an excited yelp. 'The beast!' she exclaimed. 'You haven't told me about the beast, Nicola. Who is he? What has he done to deserve his reputation? And most important of all, is he handsome?'

The frown returned to Nicola's brow and Liz half regretted asking her about him, but could not conceal the eager curiosity which consumed her as she waited impatiently for an answer.

Nicola swallowed her anger and made a great effort to calm herself. The very name Matt Devlin seemed to agitate her strongly, and Liz's curiosity was whetted anew as she noted her struggle for composure. She swallowed hard, her green eyes emerald bright as she answered with a bitterness totally alien to her nature.

'Handsome? Oh, yes, he is handsome, I believe. A handsome black devil typical of generations of Devlins before him! And with his full quota of their inherent characteristics, I've no doubt. Treacherous, vindictive, and overbearingly conceited!'

Liz gave out a slow breath of amazement. She waited for more, but Nicola seemed to be struggling inwardly to suppress the agitation that her outburst had aroused within her and she had to prompt her.

'But what has he *done*, Nicola? You surely can't have come into contact with him for the past few years or you would have mentioned him to me before now. Is it something to do with your family?' She waited wonderingly for her reply.

Nicola stood up hurriedly and began to pace around the room. When she spoke it was as if her thoughts were attempting to keep up with the quickness of her steps and the words tumbled past her lips in a flood of pent-up emotion.

'The Devlins were responsible for my parents' death!' She hesitated for a moment and then with intrinsic fairness she added, 'At least, the father was . . . But I can assure you that the son is capable of being as beastly as his father. Doesn't his action in dismissing Dulcie prove that he's just as arrogant and unfeeling?'

She swung round to challenge Liz with this statement, daring her to contradict, and her friend swallowed the words of possible vindication which she had been about to speak on the unfortunate Matt Devlin's behalf and contented herself with a weak, 'But are you sure, Nicola? You were very young when your parents died, perhaps you misunderstood something you overheard? Oughtn't you to be very sure of your facts before condemning him so unmercifully?' She warmed to her theme as she detected uncertainty on Nicola's face. 'How can you possibly know that he's as black as he's painted? Or even, for that matter, that his father is?'

Nicola's face hardened. She stopped her pacing and sat down again in the deep armchair that she had vacated a few moments before; but not to relax. She was as tense as a coiled spring as she sat twisting her fingers into knots thinking of the tragedy that had blighted her childhood. She answered Liz's question with another.

'Sure of my facts? Of course I'm sure! Aunt Sarah told me the story so many times that I know it off by heart.'

Mercifully, she missed the look of disgust that chased across Liz's face at the mention of her Aunt Sarah and continued to speak.

'It seems,' she choked, 'that at one time my mother

and Matt Devlin's father were very good friends; more than friends, for he wanted to marry her. They were both young and unattached and there were very few young people in the vicinity at that time, so it was quite a natural thing that they should go about together. There was never any sort of understanding between them, at least not on my mother's part, and when my father went to work at Scaur Bank Mills for Charles Devlin's father and met and fell in love with my mother, and she with him, she felt quite free to accept his proposal, for she had never at any time allowed Charles Devlin to think that there could ever be anything but friendship between them. However,' she went on hardly, 'Charles Devlin didn't think the same! As soon as he was told that they were to be married he almost went berserk. At first he went to see my mother and demanded that she give up the idea of marrying anyone but himself, and when she refused he threatened to do everything in his power to spoil their marriage. My mother just ignored his threats—she didn't even mention them to my father, just to Aunt Sarah—and went ahead with the wedding.'

Nicola's young face went peaked and her beautiful green eyes looked enormous as she dwelt upon the horror of the tale, as she had been told it. As if mesmerized, she carried on.

'Charles Devlin kept his word! From the day of the wedding he persecuted my father in every way possible. He made his life unbearable at the mill, going to unbelievable lengths to put him in the wrong with *his* father, who at that time had the running of the works, Charles merely being his understudy, and what's more natural than for a father to take his son's word before that of an employee? Even an employee who had proved his worth as a brilliant designer, as my father had? Eventually, things got so bad that my father could take no more.

He applied for another post in a town miles away from Carswell, and got it. It was when he and my mother were returning from the town where he was to work, after having been to see the house where we were to live, that the accident happened. They were both killed outright when a lorry pulled out in front of their car. And if Charles Devlin had had the decency to leave them alone they would both be alive today!'

Liz was horrified. The idea of any man being cruel enough to deliberately try to break up the marriage of two happy young people sickened her, and she held out her hand to Nicola in unspoken sympathy. Nicola took it gratefully and for a moment they sat in silence, Liz trying to find words to express her commiseration and Nicola endeavouring to stem the tide of bitterness that washed over her each time she thought of the tragic and unnecessary death of her parents.

Liz cleared her throat. The swift rush of compassion she felt when she heard the reason for her friend's antipathy towards the Devlin family was followed by a faint doubt born of an instinctive distrust of Nicola's informant. Although she had no reason to think Sarah Dawson would lie to her niece she could not shake off a feeling of doubt as to whether all that she said could be treated as gospel. Little slips of the tongue that pointed to the fact that Sarah could stretch a fact to embellish a story to her own glorification were recalled by Liz from the time that she had spent the weekend with the Dawsons, and for some unaccountable reason she felt bound to put in a plea for the luckless Matt Devlin.

'Charles Devlin must be an absolute rotter, darling. But do you think it's quite fair to blame his son for his father's black deeds? Some sons are quite different from their fathers, you know. Isn't it possible that it might be so in this case?'

Nicola turned incredulous eyes on her.

'But isn't it enough that he's played such a dirty trick upon Dulcie? What more proof do you need that he's a true Devlin? Don't spare any sympathy for him, Liz! Nothing you can say will convince me that he's any different from his father!'

Liz gave up. With a shrug of her shoulders she indicated that she had tried and failed and that she was now retiring to a neutral corner.

The small clock on the table by the window chimed suddenly and brought home to them the fact that the evening had almost reached its limitations, and as they were both conscious of fatigue they began simultaneously to gather up the remains of their meal and to stack the dishes in the tiny sink in the diminutive kitchenette. They had agreed, when they had first moved into their flat, that being as constricted as it was life would be made unbearable unless they made it a rule to clear up any clutter and general untidiness each evening before they retired to bed. They had been tempted many times to break this rule, especially after a late night or a particularly heavy day, but had managed doggedly to resist the temptation to leave it until the following morning, with the result that now it had become force of habit to leave their kitchen spotless, the couch and armchairs free from magazines and newspapers, and all outdoor clothes and shoes put away tidily in their respective cupboards.

Liz did the tidying up while Nicola washed the few dishes they had used at supper. When she had finished, she carefully rinsed out the sink and put away the precious china. She stepped into the living-room where Liz was having a final cigarette before going to bed and accepted one from the packet she tossed towards her as an invitation for Nicola to join her.

There was a very strong bond of affection between the two girls. Liz had no family of her own to take her troubles to, and she had found in Nicola a substitute for the sister she had always longed for. Vivacious and excitable as she was, the serene and capable nature of her flatmate worked like a charm on her sometimes tattered nerves, often shredded by the unreasonable demands of capricious photographers untiring in their demands for more and still more shots for their insatiable cameras. Many an evening she had come home and poured out her resentment to a receptive and sympathetic Nicola, to be calmed down almost to purring point by her soothing presence and almost infallible potion for all crises—a cup of tea.

Now the shoe was on the other foot and she felt herself inadequate in her desire to comfort and advise. She was worried about Nicola's blindness to the guile of the Dawson family and desperately wanted to warn her against being taken in by them. She desisted, not because of any qualms regarding Sarah or Dulcie Dawson, but because she knew only too well that the fanatical loyalty Nicola felt towards her relatives could well result in their having a difference of opinion that might cause a definite breach between them, and that she could not— would not—risk.

Nicola smiled as she glanced towards Liz and saw the worried pucker between her brows. She leaned over and patted her gently on her arm. With her usual perception she had guessed what was behind it.

'Don't worry about me, my pet. I'll be perfectly all right. I'm not going for ever, you know, just for a couple of days.'

Liz took her up on this statement. With an almost pitiful plea in her voice she pledged her.

'Promise? You *will* come back in a few days, won't you, Nicola? Promise me?'

Nicola looked at her in amazement. 'But of course I will! I've told you I've no intention of staying. I'll be back in less than a week.'

Liz looked a trifle shamefaced and tried to dispel the fears that had come unbidden to her mind. Hesitantly, she tried to explain.

'It's just that I've a feeling that this visit will be a turning point in your life, Nicola. I can't explain, but somehow I feel that our partnership is at an end and I can't bear the thought of having to share this flat with anyone else. I've a premonition that tonight will be the last night we'll spend together here.'

There were tears in her eyes as she said this and Nicola looked at her in bewilderment.

'You silly goose!' she reprimanded her. 'Come along, it's time you were in bed. I absolutely refuse to listen to any more of this silly nonsense.'

She led the still tearful Liz to her bedroom door and gave her a playful push.

'Good night, goose!'

Liz gave her a swift hug and closed her door.

CHAPTER II

THE cold impersonality of the towering steel and glass cathedral that was Carswell Railway Station could not chill the warmth of homecoming that had enveloped Nicola from the moment she had boarded the train at St. Pancras. She sniffed appreciatively at the familiar smells that transported her back to her childhood days when her father, at her instigation, had brought her here as a special treat to see the trains coming and going and to watch the endless streams of people with their luggage, magazines, and handbags, all in a seemingly terrific hurry to get to unknown and terribly exciting places.

Now *she* was one of those people, and had been for some years now, but the same sense of urgency still communicated itself to her as in days gone by as she picked up her suitcase from the platform and joined the throng, tickets in hands, that was making its way to the barriers.

She was not expecting to be met, for she had not informed her aunt of her imminent arrival. She had explained to Liz that she would be at her aunt's house almost as soon as a letter, providing she caught the first available train, and this she had done.

Her boss had been surprisingly meek when confronted by her demand for a week's holiday. She had been prepared to do battle and had a list of previously prepared arguments to counteract any objections which he might put forward, but, to her astonishment, his reaction had been one of pained resignation and a grudging acceptance that what had to be had to be. Even the fact that she wanted her holiday to start immediately had not brought forth the wrath to which she had steeled herself, and she had found herself outside the office door with her holiday pay in her hand and his strict injunction to remember that the Christmas rush was almost upon them and to return in good time prepared to do battle with the backlog of work which her absence was almost certain to cause ringing in her ears.

She stepped out of the station entrance into what was known as Citadel Square. Immediately, she was engulfed by the familiar swell of pride which never failed to assail her at the sight of the majestic twin towers of the Citadel—first built in the reign of Henry VIII and rebuilt some two hundred and fifty years ago—which now served as Court Houses to the historic and ancient borough of Carswell.

The old town was soaked in history. Nicola loved to wander through what was left of the old part of the city, along the remnants of the Roman wall, built to withstand the attacks of marauding Scots, and to stand and drink in the beauty of the sweetly mellowed stone of the great castle that stood like a sentinel watching over the bustling activity of the city it had nurtured from infancy, then to wander along for a further few yards to be confronted by the solemn grandeur of Carswell Cathedral, renowned throughout the land for the sublime beauty of its stained-glass window.

She hesitated in front of the taxi rank and then decided. She turned on her heel and walked back into the station to leave her suitcase at the Left Luggage office, to be collected later. With a slight feeling of guilt, for she knew that by rights she should have hurried to her aunt without the least delay, she walked out of the station once more, past the taxi rank, and joined the swell of busy shoppers who were oblivious, owing no doubt to familiarity, to the romance and sense of unfolding history that was all around them.

Each time Nicola visited her home town she was dismayed to find yet another new building taking up the space occupied at one time by an old and well-loved monument to the architects of yesteryear. This time, the dusty but exciting jumble of her favourite antique shop had been replaced by a glittering façade that proclaimed itself to be 'Angela's Boutique' and she had to quicken her steps and avert her gaze from the monstrosity so as to subdue her urge to pick up a brick and hurl it through the ornamented, characterless mass of plate-glass window.

The sight saddened her terribly and the expectant urge to explore her beloved town receded, leaving her feeling the effects of her hurried departure from London and the strain of her long journey. Suddenly she wanted no more than to get home to her aunt's house where there would be a welcome cup of tea and a glowing fire to chase away the distinct chill which was beginning to creep over her. She caught sight of a large red bus standing at the traffic lights, it was bound in her direction, so she nipped smartly up to the bus stop at the side of Woolworth's sprawling edifice and heaved a sigh of relief as it drew up just as she reached the stop. Within minutes they were leaving the hub of the city and as Nicola peered eagerly out of the bus window she saw in the distance a great mass of grey merging with clouds on the far horizon that indicated to those who knew the geography of the town that the lakes and fells of the Lake District were a mere fifteen miles to the south of the city.

Her aunt's house was part of the Devlin property. It stood apart from the Mill itself and was enclosed on three sides by sturdy trees that effectively screened the sprawling works buildings, and the more modern office block that flanked it, from its sight. Matt Devlin's grandfather had built it for his own use at the beginning of the century, together with other smaller dwellings for his key workers, but the family had long outgrown it and had moved to a splendid residence some miles away, isolated from the sound of the scurrying feet of the workers as they hastened to answer the call of the works hooter at seven-thirty each morning, and from the cease-less throbbing of the machines that turned out the miles of material destined for the fashion houses of the world. Devlin's Mills were world-famous for the quality and design of their merchandise and, even in these days of cut-throat competition, could hold their own with any in their own sphere.

Nicola stepped off the bus at its terminus and turned right, away from the works, towards a path which skirted the works' bowling green on one side, and the fast-flowing River Carswell on the other. A fairly large metal bridge gave access to the mill from the workers' houses on the other side of the river, and Nicola had to admit, albeit grudgingly, that the Devlin family had certainly done well by their workers in giving them such a lovely spot in which to live. One just had to turn one's eyes away from the mill and the cluster of houses and shops that had grown up over the years to supply the workers' needs, and face south, to be confronted by the sight of miles of grazing land, dotted with cattle and trees, that stretched as far as the eye could see. Through the lush green fields the river rushed, or flowed, according to its mood and the state of the elements, to terminate in a waterfall which was the delight of all the children in the neigh-bourhood. Nicola herself had spent many happy hours playing at the side of the thundering fall, and later, when she was able to swim, she had dived with delight from the top of the fall and into the deep pool that made it a natural bathing spot during the summer months.

Even her aunt had been heard to admit on one occasion that the site could not be bettered, having as it did the convenience of a bus service which enabled one to reach the town in a matter of five minutes and, on the other hand, the delights of the countryside at one's doorstep. The fact that this praise had been given in an effort to impress one of her friends who had had the audacity to pity her for having to live so near to a factory made it no less the truth. And the fact that she and her family had for years been living rent free was another reason why Sarah Dawson would never dream of moving. Her husband, who had been manager at the mill for many years, had, by grace of his position and the length of his service, been entitled to one of the staff houses, and when offered the house vacated by the Devlins, had accepted gratefully. But Nicola, although aware that the house belonged to the firm, had no idea that it was free, nor indeed had anyone else. The common practice was for the tenant to pay a nominal sum, however small, but Sarah had never disclosed to any of her cronies that, far from being the expense she had more than once implied, it was costing her nothing to live in the classically built domain that had been destined, initially, for the Devlin family.

Nicola's steps quickened automatically as her ears picked up the sound of the muted roar of the waterfall. She rounded the clump of shrubs and evergreens that shielded her aunt's house from sight and stopped suddenly to drink in the view, the memory of which had sustained her throughout her years in London and of which she could never tire of looking.

Far in the distance she could see, towering above the low green hills and groups of sturdy trees that gave shelter to the cattle that grazed peacefully in the river valley, the majestic snow-capped Cumberland fells. They stood out clearly on the horizon, seeming to beckon to the town-weary Nicola to drop everything and to hasten out to them to discover the freedom and glorious sense of tranquillity that she never failed to find there.

Her glance lingered longingly until a movement near at hand brought her back to earth. Two magnificent white swans glided royally into sight from out of a den of willows that overhung the grassy bank of the river. To Nicola this put the seal upon her homecoming, for as long as she could remember, the swans had put in an appearance each year on the same stretch of river. She had fed them, crusts clenched in an eager little fist, since childhood, and the sight of them brought a lump to her throat and a wave of nostalgia for the pitifully short period of happiness she had enjoyed with her parents threatened to overwhelm her.

She gave a determined shake and turned to the right, away from the fall, to walk towards her aunt's house. She opened the iron trellised gate to step on to the short drive that led to the front door and immediately heard a frantic barking and a hurried scuffling. She waited expectantly. A second later a furious bundle of dog came rushing round from the back of the house and hurled itself in front of her. It skidded to a stop almost at her feet, its ears pricked up and coat bristling with rage. Nicola laughed out loud and put out her hand to give it an affectionate cluff on the head.

'Rufus, you old silly! It's only me. Don't tell me you've forgotten me?'

The golden-coated Labrador reacted to her voice with a whimper of delight. He immediately rolled over on his back, paws in the air, and almost begged her to tickle him. Then, before she could oblige, he jumped up again in a frenzy of joy and put his great paws on her shoulders and slobbered over her with much feeling.

'Down, Rufus!' she ordered him, laughingly. 'Down, good dog!'

As she tried to brush some of the mud from his paws off her coat the front door opened swiftly and her aunt's voice startled her as its shrill tones penetrated above the noise of the dog who was still barking his delight.

'Nicola! Have you brought her back? Where is she? Oh, my poor baby!'

Sarah Dawson saw the bewilderment on Nicola's face. Her voice sharpened with anxiety.

'Where's Dulcie? Haven't you brought her back with you?'

Nicola shook her head. 'I'm sorry, Aunt Sarah, but I haven't a clue what you're talking about. Hadn't we better go inside and then you can explain?'

Her aunt wrung her hands with impotent anxiety, but stood aside to let Nicola into the house before carrying on with her lament. Nicola ushered her into the small sitting-room which had windows overlooking the fall and pushed her gently into an armchair. As her aunt was about to speak she forestalled her by saying firmly:

'Not another word, Aunt Sarah, until I've made you a cup of tea. You look exhausted. Just sit there quietly, it won't take me a minute, and then you can tell me the whole story.'

Sarah allowed herself to be fussed over and gave Nicola a rather wan smile as she settled herself back in her chair with a self-pitying sigh. In a matter of minutes Nicola was back with a tray and when she had poured out the reviving liquid and handed a cup to her aunt, who took it with alacrity, she asked her gently:

'Now, suppose you tell me where Dulcie is supposed to be, and why you thought I should have brought her back?'

Sarah gave a self-pitying gulp and groped in her pocket for a moment without answering. Without a word, she handed Nicola a note from out of her pocket and sat sipping her tea while she waited to see her niece's reaction after reading it.

It was terse and to the point. Dulcie had obviously

given little thought to her mother's peace of mind when she had written it, for all it contained were bare facts. Nicola looked at the words Dulcie had penned in obvious haste.

Gone to London to stay with Nicola. Can't stand this place another minute. Will write. Dulcie.

Nicola felt a slow burning anger begin to smoulder inside her as she read the pitifully few words. Anger, not against Dulcie, even though she did deserve to be chastised for leaving her mother in such a way, but against Matt Devlin, who was the cause of Dulcie's unhappiness and the reason for her precipitous flight. Her face was flushed with anger, but she purposely made her voice light when she asked her aunt :

'When did she leave?'

Sarah put down her cup with trembling fingers and wiped a tear from her eye. 'She must have left last night and caught the midnight train, or she could have gone by bus, I don't know,' she quavered. 'She was in her room for best part of the day yesterday, probably packing. Then she went out for an hour after tea, then watched television with me until ten o'clock. We had a light supper and I went to bed about half an hour later. That,' she began to cry now in earnest, 'was the last I saw of her. Oh, Nicola!' she turned her tear-filled eyes to Nicola, 'how could she treat me in this way? Her own mother!'

'And she's told you nothing more about the circumstances under which she left the factory?'

A furtive glance sped from under Sarah's eyelids as she gave a swift denial. 'No, not another word. I'm as much in the dark as you are.'

Nicola made a swift calculation and jumped up to go towards the telephone which stood on a small table by the window. Sarah watched her questioningly as she dialled a number and while she waited to be connected Nicola told her :

'We must obviously have passed each other on our journeys, and Dulcie would find no one at home when she reached the flat, for Liz had an early appointment this morning and would be out when she called. I'm ringing through to the flat. Liz should have arrived home by now and I can ask her if she's had any word of Dulcie.'

As she finished speaking the receiver was lifted at the other end and Liz's slight drawl could be heard giving her number.

'Liz, thank goodness you're in ! This is Nicola speaking.'

'Nicola ! This is nice ! I've just got in to an empty flat, worn out and weary and full of woe, thinking how nice it would be to hear your cheery voice when *voilà!* you ring me up. How are things going up in the frozen north? And when can I expect you back? I'll kill the fatted calf, darling, and have everything clean and shiny for your return.'

'Liz,' Nicola broke in, 'things are a bit difficult here. I didn't ring you up just to hear the sound of your voice, sweet though it is. I want to ask you if you've seen or heard anything of Dulcie.'

'Dulcie? Why should you think I would know anything about Dulcie?'

'Because when I arrived home Aunt Sarah was terribly upset. Dulcie went off last night leaving a note to say she was going to contact me in London. I thought perhaps she had been to the flat and that you might have talked with her.'

'Oh, dear !' Liz's voice was full of sympathy for Nicola. 'I'm afraid I've just this minute arrived home. If she *has* been here she wouldn't get an answer. Perhaps she'll call later this evening. I have a date, but as this is so important I'll break it and stay in in case she calls, and if she does I'll ring you back immediately. Will that do?'

'Thank you, Liz. You're a real brick! That'll put Aunt Sarah's mind at rest.'

'Think nothing of it, darling,' Liz answered. 'I'm not awfully keen on my date, anyway, so it's not such a great sacrifice. 'Bye for now!'

Nicola put down the phone with a sigh of relief and told her aunt briefly what Liz had promised to do. Sarah's eyes brightened a little at the news and Nicola felt a swift compassion for her as she noted the dark circles around her washed-out blue eyes. She put an arm around her shoulders and coaxed her gently.

'Why don't you go upstairs and lie down for a while, Aunt Sarah? I'll call you if Liz rings back before you awake. I'm sure it'll do you good to have a nap.'

Sarah acquiesced gratefully and stood up to do as she was bid. Nicola helped her up the stairs to her bedroom and when she had seen that she was comfortable went back downstairs to the sitting-room and sat down in her favourite chair at the window overlooking the waterfall. Dusk had crept up unawares and all she could see was the faint outlines of the shrubs in the garden, but even through the closed doors and windows she could hear the faint sound of the waterfall as thousands of gallons of water from the swiftly flowing river gushed along between the river banks and over the edge of the dam to fall in a frothy foaming cascade into the bay below.

She leaned her head back on a cushion and closed her eyes as weariness washed over her, but as she snuggled down in her chair to try to woo sleep thoughts and problems whirled through her mind with frantic speed until she finally gave up all thought of sleep and sat deliberating on the almost insoluble problem of what to do about her aunt and her cousin Dulcie. As her hand drummed restlessly upon her knee she felt a cold nose pushed into it and looked down to see a pair of brown liquid orbs gazing lovingly at her. Absent-mindedly, she fondled the dog's silky head, and he whimpered his delight and pressed his heavy body closer to her legs.

'Poor Rufus,' she murmured. 'I don't suppose anyone has bothered to take you for a good run since I was here last, have they, old son? Never mind, I promise I'll take you for a good walk before I go back to London.'

Rufus wagged his tail slowly, as if understanding that her mind was occupied with more pressing problems than his, and put a sympathetic paw on her knee.

For more than an hour she sat, deep in thought, fighting the inevitability of the only solution that had presented itself to her. Her mind weighed and rejected alternative courses to the one that was distasteful to her until she was left with no other choice but to face the cold fact that if Dulcie was determined to stay in London then she, Nicola, would have to remain in Carswell with Aunt Sarah! Not that she was averse to living in the lovely old town. And even if she were, the close proximity of her beloved Lake District would have more than compensated her. But to have to leave the job which she loved and enjoyed doing and, more especially, to have to leave Liz and the flat, was a course too painful to think about.

Her reverie was brought to an abrupt end as the telephone shrilled its summons through the quiet room, causing both Nicola and the dog to jump with alarm. She ran to pick up the receiver and heard Liz's voice at the other end.

'Nicola?'

'Yes, Liz. Have you heard anything?'

To Nicola's ears Liz's voice sounded rather dry as she answered her in the affirmative.

'Yes, dear, she's here, safe and sound. She didn't call

at the flat immediately she arrived but has been looking up some friends of hers here in London. By all accounts she's had a marvellous day with them, but as they can't put her up she's called here to find a bed for the night and to ask if she can stay until she finds somewhere to live. Hold on a minute and I'll put her on the line.'

Nicola took the opportunity, while Liz exchanged places with Dulcie, to call up the stairs to her aunt, and was thankful to see her coming out of her bedroom, the sound of the telephone having wakened her from her doze. She mimed to her as she picked up the phone once more, to indicate that Dulcie was safe, and her aunt gave a sigh of relief at the message. She moved forward eagerly to take the phone from Nicola's hand, but hesitated when she heard Dulcie's voice asking for her cousin.

'Nicola?'

'Yes, Dulcie, I'm here. And I'm waiting for an explanation! What do you mean by causing your mother such distress? I really can't see why you couldn't have let her know you were leaving home instead of going off in secret as you did. You must have known she'd be worried to death!'

Dulcie's sulky voice answered her. 'You know as well as I do that she would've made an unholy fuss and refused to let me go. It was the only way. I've no intention of coming back home yet, so you can tell her that; and nothing that either of you may say will make me change my mind!'

Nicola recoiled from the harsh unfeeling tone of her cousin's voice as she stated her intention of remaining in London and turned away from her aunt as if to shield her from the hurtful decree. But Sarah had heard, Nicola realized, for she sank down on the nearest chair with a low moan and covered her face with her hands. She tried to reason with Dulcie.

'But what about your mother? You know she can't

be left alone, her health isn't good—and besides that, she's nervous of being left alone in the house.'

'Then why don't you stay, Nicola?' Dulcie's mocking voice asked her. 'You owe her that much, surely. If it hadn't been for her you would never have known a home of your own. I should think,' she jibed, 'you'd welcome the opportunity of repaying her kindness to you.'

There was the sound of indignant altercation at the other end of the phone and Nicola was startled out of her silence by the sound of Liz's furious voice humming over the wires.

'No, Nicola, you mustn't take any notice of her! Your place is here in London with me and your friends. And what about your job? You can't let them down at the agency, they're expecting you back at the end of the week. Please, Nicola, say you'll be coming back!'

But even as she pleaded, Nicola knew what she had to do. This was the solution she had come to while waiting for the phone call and, even then, she had known it was the only way. She took a deep breath and prepared to do battle with Liz. She had to convince her friend that this was the only solution and she knew it would take all her powers of persuasion to get her to see it her way.

After almost a quarter of an hour of pleading she managed, by dint of implacable determination, to convince her that there was no other alternative until, finally, Liz gave in with a bad grace, still insisting that Nicola's place was in London with her. She consented, making it plain, however, that it was only to oblige Nicola, to let Dulcie stay on in the flat until she was prepared to go back home, and agreed—reluctantly—to go with her to the agency the following morning to explain the situation and to help to persuade Mr. Harding to find a place for Dulcie on his staff. She bade Nicola an almost tearful goodbye and pledged her to write every week and to return to London at the earliest possible opportunity. This

Nicola gladly promised to do, and there was a lump in her throat as she put down the phone and turned to her aunt, who had heard most of the conversation and was beaming with satisfaction at the news that Nicola was to stay with her.

The thought that both her Aunt Sarah and Dulcie were rather selfishly insistent on having things their own way came unbidden to Nicola and was hastily pushed out of her mind almost before the thought had crystallized. She set out to be especially pleasant to Sarah in an effort to compensate for the treacherous thought and her aunt blossomed under her solicitude. She prattled on about the things they would do and the people they would visit, and when she had arranged their social life for weeks ahead, sat contentedly watching television while Nicola prepared their supper.

It didn't enter her head to wonder what Nicola would do about getting a job, but this was the problem Nicola was grappling with as she pottered about in the old-fashioned kitchen, setting out their supper-tray.

Quite suddenly it came to her. Why not? She could kill two birds with one stone and not only find herself employment but perhaps discover the reason for Dulcie's dismissal. She would go tomorrow to Scaur Bank Mills and apply for the job from which Dulcie had been so summarily dismissed. Secretary to the boss of the mill, Matt Devlin!

CHAPTER III

NICOLA almost danced out of the personnel office of Scaur Bank Mills. She had done it! She had landed the job of personal secretary to Matt Devlin and was to start work almost immediately.

As they had had much difficulty in filling the position, really qualified secretaries being thin on the ground in that part of the country, Nicola's formidable qualifications had clinched the matter without any hesitation, and the personnel officer, Miss Sendall, had welcomed her with pathetic eagerness.

On asking, and being reassured, that Nicola could start the next day, she had heaved a sigh of relief and a beam of satisfaction had chased away the slightly harassed look that Nicola had noted at the beginning of her interview. As she had got up to leave, Miss Sendall had asked her in a slightly hesitant manner :

'Er . . . one thing more, Miss Brent.'

Nicola had turned questioningly and to her surprise saw a faint colour staining Miss Sendall's cheeks which had seemed to denote embarrassment. She waited for her to go on.

'I must ask you, Miss Brent. Are you used to working for a boss who is . . .' she seemed to find difficulty in choosing her words, 'shall we say . . . rather temperamental? I don't mean,' she hurried on, 'that he's an excitable or bad-tempered man. It's just that . . . well, he doesn't suffer fools gladly, I'm afraid.'

At Nicola's raised eyebrows and look of hauteur she had amended her remark hastily.

'Oh, forgive me, Miss Brent. I didn't mean that the

way it sounded. I'm not suggesting for a moment that you're a fool,' her face was by then a bright shade of crimson, 'I just meant to convey the impression that young Mr. Devlin is a stickler for efficiency. But there,' she stumbled on, 'I'm sure you are everything a busy man could possibly require in a secretary.'

Nicola had taken pity on her then, and instead of sweeping out of the office with disdain, as she would have been quite entitled to do after the rather incompetent picture that had been painted of her, she had earned Miss Sendall's gratitude by smiling down at her and saying with a rather enigmatical smile :

'Please don't worry. I assure you I can handle Mr. Devlin, whatever his moods. I'll make it my personal responsibility to ensure that he gets everything he deserves !'

Miss Sendall's rather weak-looking grey eyes had blinked nervously behind her spectacles at this rejoinder and the smile of satisfaction had become a trifle uncertain as she detected the small note of disparity in Nicola's voice, but she had shrugged her shoulders and decided that the pressure she had been under from Mr. Matt to get him a secretary immediately had tired her even more than she had thought possible and that her imagination was probably working overtime.

Nicola braced herself subconsciously as she prepared to confront her Aunt Sarah with her news. She wouldn't be pleased to hear that all her planned visits would have to be cancelled and still less pleased to learn that her niece was about to join the staff of the Devlin Mills, but it couldn't be helped. She had to have a job of some kind, so why not this one? At least it would give her the opportunity of solving the mystery of Dulcie's dismissal, and when she had sorted that out she would then be quite free to go back to her own life in London.

She began to hum to herself as she walked along the

2—TLFMD

path that led to the waterfall and her aunt's home—her home now, for as long as it took her to untangle herself from her family commitments. She could hear the sound of children's voices and their screams of delight as she passed the playground, laid out with every conceivable object that lent itself to a child's enjoyment, that had been the brain-child of another of the ancestors of the Devlin family. She frowned a little to herself as the seeming generosity of the owners of the Mill clashed in her mind with the picture of self-indulgent tyrants painted for her by her aunt. Her mind began to wrangle for a split second, but then, as a golden bundle of fur catapulted itself towards her, she pushed the vexing thought from her mind and pushed her arms out in front of her in order to hold off, albeit ineffectually, the ecstatic onslaught of Rufus whose doggy exuberance threatened to overbalance her into the swift-flowing river. She picked up a stick and threw it for him, laughing loudly at his wild scamper after it and his almost human look of pleasure as he retrieved it and laid it at her feet for her to throw once more. She obliged him readily, and they spent the next half-hour frolicking together on the river bank in front of the house.

When Nicola was almost spent and the dog's tongue was rolling with pleasurable exhaustion she heard a peevish voice calling out :

'Nicola! Where have you been? And please stop that dog from barking—he's getting on my nerves!'

Nicola turned guiltily towards her aunt and grabbed hold of Rufus's collar in an effort to subdue his vocal enjoyment.

'I'm sorry, Aunt Sarah. I'll come in now. Rufus has played long enough. Just a minute while I scrape the mud off my shoes!'

Sarah gave a delicate shudder of disgust at the sight of Nicola's shoes which were covered with thick red clay from the edge of the sodden river bank where she had gathered it when making a frantic rush in an effort to reach the stick before Rufus could dash away with it. All part of the game the pair of them had been so engrossed in, but now, as she looked down at her nearly new shoes with a grimace of dismay, she felt she deserved the censure in her aunt's voice and spoke firmly in the negative to Rufus as he tried to continue their game.

It was not until they were seated at the table for their lunch that Nicola broached the subject of going to work for Matt Devlin. Her aunt was astounded.

'Work for that man? How could you suggest such a thing, Nicola? Where is your loyalty to your cousin? To me? Not to mention your poor dead parents!'

Nicola flinched at this last remark and her aunt had the grace to look slightly ashamed. Nicola swallowed her hurt and answered her gently.

'But don't you see, Aunt Sarah? I'm taking the job for the purpose of finding out why Dulcie was dismissed. It's a wrong which can't be ignored as you and Dulcie have ignored it. I'll not rest until I've been given a satisfactory explanation for the unjust treatment meted out to her. And at the same time,' her voice hardened with purpose, 'I shall relish meeting this self-opinionated boor, and when the time is ripe I'll tell him who I am and what I think of his arbitrary manner!'

Sarah was now definitely agitated.

'No, Nicola, I forbid you to have anything to do with that man or any of his family! I absolutely forbid it, do you hear me?'

But Nicola was not to be dissuaded. 'I'm sorry, Aunt Sarah,' she stuck out her chin determinedly, 'but I've made up my mind!'

Sarah tried pleading, cajoling, and finally threatened to go to Matt Devlin to tell him what had been in her mind when she had applied for the job as his secretary,

but this was an empty threat and they both knew it.
When she realized at last that Nicola was not to be
swayed from her purpose she dissolved into tears in a last
effort to make her change her mind.

Nicola almost lost patience with her. She couldn't
understand the violent emotion that consumed her aunt.
Annoyance she had been prepared to put up with, but
her dismay was out of all proportion and Nicola was
puzzled as well as annoyed by it.

'Why do you object so strongly to my taking over the
job, Aunt Sarah? You didn't object to Dulcie doing it.
So why all this fuss?'

Sarah seemed to collapse like a pricked balloon. With
a look of unendurable pathos she rose from her seat and
walked out of the room to go upstairs to her bedroom.
Nicola heard the slam of her door as she disappeared
inside and gave a sigh of resignation. Rufus, never far
away from his beloved mistress if he could possibly help
it, moved closer to her and laid his head upon her knee
with loving sympathy. As she looked down at him she
was touched to see the dumb adoration in his great brown
eyes. She patted his head and smiled.

'You think I'm right, don't you, old son?' she questioned him. He wagged his tail madly.

'All right, you darling,' she smiled, 'you shall have your
reward. Come on, we'll go for walkies!'

She jumped up and ran to change into her favourite
walking gear so as to be comfortable when braving the
elements.

There was a strong wind whipping up the surface of
the river and the spray from the waterfall blew into her
face with icy tingles as she stood for a moment watching
the heavy volume of water frothing and seething as it fell
into the dam below. Rufus pranced and barked his impatience as she stood there fascinated, before turning
away reluctantly to follow the path that led to the open

countryside. Her steps quickened as the biting wind sought to penetrate her bright green anorak and tartan trews and she bent her head to force her way against almost solid gusts that flung themselves against her with maniacal fury.

Walking with head down, she lost sight of Rufus, and it was only when she paused for a second to shelter behind the trunk of a huge oak tree that she realized he was missing. She shouted and whistled, but the wind drowned her puny efforts. She looked around anxiously, then thought she caught a glimpse of his golden coat in the distance, just disappearing over the crest of a small hill to the left of her. She scrambled after him, head down, and gasped as the full force of the wind caught her when she breasted the hill. Involuntarily, she closed her eyes and put up her hands to pull her hood closer round her ears. It was then she ran full tilt into something hard and unyielding that caught her arms in a grip of iron.

A scream caught in her throat and was whipped away by the wind. Her long lashes flew up from her brilliant green eyes, enormous with fright, and she stared dumbfounded into the hard black gaze of the man who was holding her in his vice-like grip.

'Who are you?' she gasped, but the words were flung into the air without making themselves heard. She mouthed something again and saw him shake his head impatiently and gesticulate towards a small shack a few yards away around which Rufus was playfully chasing a magnificent dark red Irish Setter about the size of a small pony, with great gangling legs and a long feathery tail.

He held her as she stumbled across the uneven ground to the shelter and when he flung open the door of the hut and pushed her inside, away from the fury of the wind which seemed to be gathering force with every second, she leaned gratefully against the rough wall and fought desperately to regain her breath.

A match scraped and ignited; she turned towards the sound instinctively. He stood there eyeing her with sardonic humour. Dark, almost satanically good-looking, his eyes black as jet and his hair so dark it seemed to shimmer with blue lights. His skin was tanned a deep brown and the only light relief was the contrasting whiteness of his perfect teeth which were holding a cheroot negligently between them. He wasn't smiling, exactly. A glint of something that could have been humour glinted way down in his eyes, but his expression was derisive, even mocking. Nicola was at once attracted and repelled. She stood round-eyed, completely mesmerized by the dark scrutiny that came from eyes fringed by the thickest, sootiest lashes she had ever seen.

She harnessed her scattered wits and spoke with as much aplomb as she could muster.

'Thank you for rescuing me from that frightful wind, Mr. . . . ?'

He didn't answer in words, but gave her a satirical look from out of his ebony eyes. They raked her from head to foot, taking in her long slim legs in their tapering trews; her emerald-bright eyes, and the few red-gold tresses that had managed to escape the confines of her hood, and finally coming to rest on her tremulous mouth which was slightly parted, revealing small, white, even teeth.

His glance did not waver from its final resting place and she ran her tongue around lips that had gone suddenly dry as the silence seemed to grow pregnant with intent. She looked around swiftly for some means of escape from an atmosphere that was beginning to alarm her, but there was no way out other than through the door against which he was leaning.

Bravely, she braced her shoulders and with a hope that

her voice would not disgrace her by quivering when she spoke, she tried again.

'I'm sorry, I don't know your name, but I'm very grateful to you for helping me keep my feet. I thought the wind was about to throw me off balance. However, I think it's dying down a little now, so I'll be on my way.'

To her amazement, he laughed aloud. He threw back his head, the skin taut on the strong brown column of his neck, and seemed to be in the throes of genuine amusement. Nicola began to feel annoyed. It wasn't that she minded being laughed at, but his humour seemed to hold an element of barbarity which gave rise in her to a faint stirring of panic.

With head held high she walked up to him and demanded:

'Open the door, if you please. I want to go home now.'

He stopped laughing and looked down at her with narrowed eyes.

'Do you now?' he mocked her.

'Yes, I do, you . . . you . . . uncouth brute! Open that door immediately!' Nicola's temper was at white heat, her fear subdued by the force of her fury.

The sight of her flashing eyes and mutinous mouth seemed to goad him to action. Without his seeming to move, she felt his arms, tight as whipcord, enclose her and for one horrifying moment glimpsed the purpose in his black eyes. In a moment they were blotted out as his firm lips besieged hers and strangled the cry of protest she was about to utter. The onslaught was so sudden she had no time to struggle. No time, even, to register any sign of the emotions that shook her in the fraction of time his lips held her prisoner. He released her so suddenly she almost fell and she caught hold of his jacket to steady herself as the hut seemed to whirl around with sickening speed. Gradually it ceased its gyrations, and when she realized she was still hanging on to him she dropped her hands from his coat as if she had been stung and took a hasty step backwards, away from him.

He was looking down at her with a diabolical grin on his lips, and she took a deep breath before launching her scorn and disgust upon his arrogant black head.

'How dare you!' she spat. 'How dare you take advantage of a defenceless woman, you . . . unspeakable moron!'

He elevated his dark eyebrows at her choice of expression, but otherwise seemed not one whit disturbed by her outburst. He leaned negligently against the doorway of the hut and let his eyes flicker over her as she stood there rubbing furiously at her lips with her handkerchief in an effort to cleanse where his lips had touched.

'I'll see to it that you don't get away with such behaviour,' she burst out. 'I don't know who you are and I don't particularly care, but I'll remember you well enough to describe you to the first policeman I meet. It's an absolute disgrace to think an unescorted girl can't take a walk without being molested by brutes like you!'

To her furious amazement he began to laugh at this statement, and she was angered even more when he stopped laughing long enough to counter:

'Spare me the dramatics, please! I don't mind you girls having your bit of fun, but it's a bit much when a fellow can't walk his dog without some female trailing him every inch of the way. Go back to your friends and tell them about your little adventure—and make sure they understand that the next one I encounter on my solitary tramps won't get off so easily. And another thing . . . ' he went on before Nicola could indignantly interrupt, 'you might add that, while I'm flattered to be the object of so much female attention, no man worth his salt relishes anything that's offered too freely!'

With this last arrogant decree he swiftly opened the door of the hut and stepped outside, leaving her standing in open-mouthed wonder at his unbounded conceit. He whistled to the great red setter and it leaped gracefully in his wake as he strode without a backward glance over the brow of the hill. Nicola expelled her breath and tottered over to a wooden bench that ran along the side of the hut. She collapsed gratefully on to it and began to try to sort out her feelings and unravel his astounding statements.

That he did not believe he was unknown to her was obvious. His derisive look when she had asked his name was ample proof of that. But what on earth did he mean about telling her friends to keep away from him? It sounded as if he was being pestered by girls every time he took his dog for a walk. The fools! thought Nicola; what they can possibly see in him I can't imagine. Then a traitorous voice whispered, but he *is* very good-looking in a satanic way. Some girls might find his diabolically handsome face irresistible. Nicola snorted to herself. Yes, some girls would fall for the devil himself! In fact, she thought furiously, he would make a good stand-in for Old Nick. His actions were such as to make him fully deserving of comparison with the devil.

Still seething, she got up from her seat and went outside to find Rufus. To her relief, he was sitting waiting patiently for her and he wagged his tail engagingly when she appeared.

She spoke sharply to him, voicing the resentment she felt at his act of disobedience being the cause of her recent humiliation, then relented and gave his downcast head an encouraging pat to dispel his obvious dejection at being in his beloved mistress's bad books. He perked up immediately and flew ahead of her to pick up a stick, thinking to embark upon their favourite game.

But she was disappointingly abstract. Granted she

threw him the stick a couple of times, but her heart wasn't in it, he could tell, for it fell far short of her usual range and he had to nudge her hand reproachfully two or three times after retrieving it in order to remind her that he was waiting. After a while he gave up completely and wandered along the river bank, consoling himself by picking up different scents and following fresh trails, but with Nicola always within his sight.

The wind had dropped, leaving the river without a ripple to disturb its smooth surface. Bright blue sky with patches of fluffy white cloud had given way to a sullen grey blanket that had smothered the sun. It pressed down on the limp trees and branches presaging another of the sharp changes of weather that were so prevalent in the valleys that nestled beneath the Cumberland Fells. The first few fat drops of rain fell on Nicola's upturned face and she lifted it gratefully to receive them. Colour still stained her cheeks, for the force of her anger had left them burning as if with fever. The palms of her hands were sticky with sweat and her knees, now that reaction had set in, were feeling wobbly and weak.

She battled inwardly with herself, angrily denouncing the small thought that was fighting for recognition in her mind but which was being fiercely restrained from becoming tangible. It was *not* his kiss that had started this kaleidoscope of feeling inside of her! *Temper* was responsible for her flushed cheeks and trembling hands, and the fact that she had been caught unawares was the sole factor that had inaugurated the bemused, dazed feeling she was now experiencing.

She lifted up her hand to touch the lips that had felt his brutal kiss and pulled it down again quickly, angry with herself for her moment of weakness. She tried hard to bring back the feelings of resentment and distaste she had emulated so clearly to him, but they had flown, leaving her weak and strangely vulnerable to the memory of the dark stranger. For the first time she began to understand Liz's obsession with the opposite sex and ceased to wonder whether something had been left out of her make-up that had made her invulnerable to men.

When the question of whether she would ever encounter him again popped unbidden into her head, Nicola gave herself a sharp shake of condemnation and jerked out of her reverie shamefacedly. She was no better than the girls who had been the object of his scathing remarks earlier!

She looked around for Rufus and he answered her call to heel with unusual promptness. She was eyeing apprehensively the storm clouds that were gathering in full force and quickened her steps in the direction of her aunt's house which she could just see through a break in the trees far in the distance. She swept out of her head all thoughts except the one of getting home quickly and, if possible, dry. Tomorrow was her big day and she wanted no sniffles or shivers to mar the challenge of her first day as secretary to Mr. Matt Devlin. Time enough to think about the dark stranger when she had settled down to her new job and had time to dally with things of smaller import.

CHAPTER IV

NICOLA wakened the next morning with a feeling of nervous anticipation. She lay for a few moments listening to the excited chatter of the mill girls as they clattered over the metal bridge in small groups, discussing the events of the previous evening in high-pitched voices and with lots of good-natured raillery, before being enveloped by the heavy volume of sound that surrounded them in their daily work.

It was just half past seven and she was not due at the office until nine, but she sprang out of bed and wrapped herself in the folds of a quilted nylon dressing-gown before going downstairs to make her aunt and herself a cup of tea.

Rufus greeted her joyfully when she reached the kitchen and his ears pricked up hopefully as she spoke to him.

'All right, you old fraud, I know what you're after! Just give me time to make some tea and then I'll let you out for ten minutes.'

She carried the tea upstairs to her aunt's bedroom and wakened her with a cheerful 'good morning'.

There was no response from her sleeping figure, so she shook her slightly before greeting her once more.

'Good morning, Aunt Sarah! I've brought you a cup of tea. Better drink it while it's still hot.'

Sarah gave a groan and turned towards Nicola with a pathetic grimace. She looked terribly pale and worn in the morning light and did not need to lay on too much pathos when she pleaded with her niece:

'Please stay with me this morning, Nicola. I don't feel at all well.'

She pulled herself up from under the bed covers and subsided gratefully against the pillows that Nicola plumped up behind her, giving a weak smile as she did so.

Nicola felt a surge of dismay. If her aunt had decided to be ill this morning in an endeavour to prevent her from going to work then she would need all her tact and determination to avoid a scene. She looked keenly at Sarah, whose eyes flickered away from her direct gaze and wavered over the bedroom, looking at nothing in particular in order to avoid her scrutiny. She was taken by surprise when Nicola, instead of arguing, suddenly capitulated and said ruefully :

'All right, Aunt Sarah. If you don't wish me to go to work at the Mill, I won't go. I know you've been against the idea from the first and if it upsets you so much I'll phone the office and tell them to get someone else. It's just a pity,' she swept a quick glance at her aunt from under downcast lashes before dropping her bombshell, 'that I'll have to forgo my plan to buy a small car to take us about at weekends. I know how much you've always wanted a car, Aunt Sarah. It would have been a wonderful chance for us to get to Keswick to see your sister, and we could have gone as far as Southport to see Uncle Joe and Aunt Mavis; we might even have been able to stay for long weekends at holiday times. But of course,' she sighed, 'it's out of the question for me to spend my savings on a car if I've no job to go to. My money won't last for ever, unfortunately, and if I've no salary coming in then I shall have to go carefully to make it stretch out.'

She could not forgo a slight smile as she turned and saw the look of pleasurable excitement dawning on her aunt's face, and had to try hard not to laugh as Sarah suddenly jerked upright against her pillows and held out her hands with avidity.

'Oh, Nicola!' she gasped, 'what a wonderful idea. A car! I've always wanted a car!'

Her eyes sparkled with unashamed enthusiasm as she swiftly assessed the advantages to herself that being a car owner would bring.

'You'd be able to drive me to the whist drive at Plumbley and pick me up again when it finishes—you know how much I used to look forward to going there on Tuesdays, and now that the bus service has been cut, it's out of the question for me to go because it means a wait of almost half an hour after the whist drive is finished in order to get a bus home. And to visit my brother Joe would be ideal, for you know, Nicola, how the air at Southport always seems to do me so much good. Oh, yes, I think it's a marvellous idea!'

Full of eagerness, she got out of bed, her tea untouched, and began making her way to the bathroom. Nicola disguised the laugher that rose to her lips with a sudden cough as her aunt called out to her:

'I'll run your bath first, darling, and while you're getting ready I'll prepare the breakfast. We don't want you to be late on your first morning, do we?'

It was typical of Sarah to blandly ignore the objections she had so forcibly put forward only the day before and to be able to forget them completely in the excitement that filled her at the thought of the pleasurable days to come.

Nicola fell in with her aunt's wishes, and after a leisurely bath and breakfast, went to her bedroom to choose her outfit for her first meeting with her new boss. She took one or two items from her wardrobe, then discarded them as being too elegant for a Mill office. Her job in London had called for elegant clothes, for Mr. Harding had stressed that as his receptionist-cum-secretary he wished her to be an indication to prospective clients of the good taste and high standards of his firm, and had paid her a salary high enough to dress accordingly.

She finally decided upon a suit of russet brown double jersey that seemed to her to be fairly inconspicuous, and with it she chose a fine wool jumper of an unusual amber shade finished off with a necklace of a single strand of gold chain. She stepped back from her mirror to inspect the finished effect and was rather disturbed to see that instead of affecting a demure aspect the suit showed off her figure in detail and the brown shade threw the copper brightness of her hair into sharp relief. She grimaced wryly at her reflection and glanced swiftly at her watch to see if she had time to change. She hadn't. It was eight-forty-five and she still had to gather up the few personal belongings she liked to have around her in her office. She had lingered too long over breakfast, discussing at length with her aunt the type of car they would buy and how soon they would be able to have it delivered. Sarah's questions had been never-ending and Nicola's head had buzzed with the stimulated chatter. It was with relief she had made her release and escaped upstairs to her bedroom to begin to get dressed.

With a final frown at her reflection she shrugged her shoulders and swiftly gathered up the rest of her things, checking them over quickly as she ran down the stairs to make sure she had everything she required. Her aunt was still sitting at the breakfast-table and she looked up from her morning paper as Nicola took a step into the room.

'Oh, Nicola,' she began, 'just look at this car advertised in the paper. Don't you think it would be . . .'

But before she could say another word, Nicola broke in with a hurried, 'Goodbye, Aunt Sarah. I simply must rush. We'll talk about it this evening when I've more time.' With a hurried peck at Sarah's cheek, she hastened out of the room, closing her ears to her aunt's plaintive, 'But, Nicola . . . !'

She arrived at the personnel office on the stroke of nine. Miss Sendall was waiting there with a young girl of about sixteen who was sitting on the edge of her chair fumbling awkwardly with her handkerchief, her hair, and anything else within reach she could find to occupy her nervous fingers. She stood up when Miss Sendall said, 'Good morning, Miss Brent', to Nicola. Then, as she held out her hand to the young girl, she said, 'This is Jessica Morris. She's to be your junior assistant and I think you'll find her most capable. She'll tell you anything you want to know about the office routine, where things are kept, and so on. When you've settled in and have things working to your satisfaction Jessica will go back to the typing pool, unless, of course, you feel you still need her, in which case she'll stay with you permanently.'

Nicola gave the girl a sympathetic smile and held out her hand in a friendly gesture. The poor child was dumb with fright, and as she took a step towards Nicola she stumbled in her haste and had to grab hold of Miss Sendall in order to steady herself. She flushed scarlet with mortification and took a swift step backwards which plummeted her against a metal filing cabinet with a resounding crash. She looked ready to burst into tears when Miss Sendall gave her a look of resigned exasperation, but turned eyes full of gratitude upon Nicola when she stepped forward with a smile and said to her :

'How do you do, Jessica. I'm so relieved to know you'll be here to help me, for I must confess to feeling a trifle worried as to how I would manage in a strange office. But now I know you're to be my right-hand man, so to speak, I feel much more confident.'

Jessica's gamin face lit up, giving her rather dull, lack-lustre countenance a flash of animation that lasted for a mere second before being hidden once more by a mask of stolid withdrawal. Nicola sighed to herself, hoping that she was not to be landed with an unco-operative junior on her first morning, for she felt the job itself presented enough of a challenge without the added complication of having to placate a seemingly unsociable companion.

Miss Sendall beamed upon them both and instructed Jessica to take Nicola to her office immediately so that she would have time to prepare for Mr. Devlin who, she volunteered, would not be arriving until ten o'clock that morning.

Nicola heard this with relief. She would have half an hour at least in which to settle in before being con-fronted by the man she half dreaded meeting. In half an hour she would be face to face with the son of Charles Devlin, the monster responsible for the death of her be-loved parents; the person who throughout her young life she had regarded as a bogey-man; a wrecker of happiness, a devil incarnate! And his son, whom she was about to meet, seemed set fair to be his worthy successor.

Jessica guided her, without a word, through a laby-rinth of passages accompanied as they walked by the constant tapping of dozens of typewriters and the muffled voices of the occupants of the various offices that lined the corridors. After a few minutes, the tapping grew fainter and the interior slightly more opulent as they left the general offices behind and entered the region of the directors' quarters. Here there was luxurious pile carpet under their feet and rich dark graining on the heavy doors, each one with a highly polished handle and a small brass plate giving the occupier's name and designation. They passed a large glass door with steps leading up to it from the outside, which was obviously the main entrance to the directors' quarters—Nicola and Jessica having approached them internally and from the back—and then they mounted a small staircase that led to another floor with only two doors set in the whole length of the corridor. They had arrived! The first door had a nameplate that denoted it belonged to Mr. Devlin, Snr., and the next one, which Jessica opened and then stood back to allow Nicola to precede her, staid, stark and un-compromising—Mr. Matthew Devlin.

Nicola walked into the room and was struck immed-iately by its air of subdued comfort. The walls were colour-washed in a restful shade of green that melted into the muted blue of the superb wall-to-wall carpet. Two desks, complete with typewriters and tape recorders, were placed on either side of a large window which was draped with curtains in a decorative pattern of blue and soft green on a white background. The ceiling was white, and as she looked up she saw ephemeral ripples and swirls floating hither and thither on the matt surface as the brilliant winter sunshine danced upon the water of the river outside the window and cast its playful reflec-tion upon the ceiling which made a perfect screen. She caught her breath and stepped lightly over to the window. Sure enough, there was her favourite view. Directly below was the swathe of green that led to the river's edge. The two swans were regally dipping their grace-ful elongated necks into the swiftly flowing river as it sparkled and danced its way between the banks, to be impelled over the edge of the waterfall in a frothy spate to give the adjacent factory the benefit of its thunderous power by generating its own electricity. Her eyes left the pulsating dam and wandered over the meadows where the placidly munching cows lent grace and con-tentment to the rural scene, and then she lifted up her eyes to the hills expectantly, and was not disappointed. Far in the distance, but with visibility as it was, seeming almost near enough to touch, stood Skiddaw, Carrick and High Pike, their peaks still drowned with snow and looking unbelievably lovely against a blue, cloudless sky.

A nervous cough brought her back to earth and she turned to see Jessica holding open a door which led into another room next to the one in which they were standing.

'This is Mr. Matt's office, Miss Brent.'

Nicola moved forward towards Jessica and voiced her surprise.

'Oh, I thought this was his room, Jessica. Don't tell me he has a suite of offices?'

Jessica stood shuffling her feet, too embarrassed to talk, and waited until Nicola repeated her question before bringing herself to answer.

'Yes, Miss Brent. This office is yours and mi . . . is yours. And the one through there is Mr. Matt's.'

She followed Nicola into the second, larger office and stood once again without speaking until Nicola had surveyed the room. The smaller office which was to be Nicola's was most comfortable and quite adequately furnished even for a director, but this larger office was more like the study of a private house. Nothing had been spared either in décor or furnishing to spell out utter comfort and luxury. It was a man's room, without a doubt, for in one corner stood, incongruously, fishing rods and tackle, and in another was a set of golf clubs and a menacing-looking rifle. The walls were lined with books, hundreds of them, and placed strategically at the side of a simulated coal-effect fire was a black leather settee, sumptuously upholstered, and all of seven feet long. Nicola noted with relief that a large businesslike desk took up what was left of the floor space and that it was piled high with papers indicating, she fervently hoped, that a great deal of work was to be done, for Nicola could not stand the type of boss whose surroundings gave the impression of great activity but whose actual output was nil.

She walked thoughtfully back into her own office and Jessica followed, closing the door behind them. As she began to unbutton her coat, the door from the passage-way opened, after a slight tattoo on the panels, and a cheerful face was popped round the door.

'May I come in?'

Nicola gave a pleased smile. 'Please do. I was be-ginning to wonder if any other souls besides Jessica and myself were allowed in this sanctum.'

She liked what she saw of the pleasant-faced woman who was unashamedly assessing her and waited with benign amusement for her new acquaintance to introduce herself, it being a waste of time to expect Jessica to per-form this small service as she had once again frozen into her shell.

'I'm Edith Stern,' the woman said, proffering her hand. 'May I be one of the first to welcome you to Scaur Bank Mills? I hope you'll enjoy working with us. I'm Mr. Charles's secretary, by the way, and if there is anything I can do for you please don't hesitate to let me know.'

'Why, thank you, Miss Stern. That's most kind of you, and I'll certainly take you up on that if I'm stuck with anything that Jessica can't help me with.'

'Oh, please, not Miss Stern! Call me Edith. I do dislike to be formal and as we shall be seeing quite a lot of each other we may as well start as we mean to go on, don't you agree?'

Nicola was not given to impulsive overtures of friend-ship, preferring rather to let an acquaintanceship flower gradually and so mature into strong and lasting amity, but she recognized the sense of Edith's statement and agreed willingly.

'All right, then, Edith. And thank you.'

They smiled at each other across the room, and Nicola felt a slight lifting of the oppression she had been conscious of from the first moment she had stepped over the threshold of the Mill.

Edith walked farther into the room and Nicola took the opportunity of taking a closer look at her. She was much older than she had seemed at first glance. Her hair, although beautifully coiffured, was as white as snow and her complexion was wrinkled around the eyes and mouth by faint laughter lines that came into prominence when she smiled and gave her an aura of good-looking, tolerant maturity. She was very smartly dressed—no fuss or frills, relying upon style and perfect cut to ensure a quiet sophistication. Nicola felt an intuitive warming towards her and instinct told her she had found herself a new friend; a friend, moreover, who might prove to be a valuable ally in her quest to find out all she could about Dulcie's dismissal.

They had no time for chat, however, for no sooner had Edith settled herself in one of the chairs as a preliminary to putting Nicola wise to the vagaries of her job than the telephone shrilled its summons from Charles Devlin's office and she had to rush to answer it. She dashed back a little later to tell Nicola they would have to postpone their talk as she would be tied up for the rest of the morning, and they arranged to meet in the staff canteen at lunchtime, providing their respective bosses were finished dictating by that time and nothing else cropped up to prevent it.

Nicola had been conscious all this time that the hands of the clock were creeping steadily towards ten o'clock, and her nervousness increased with every passing minute. She took out her belongings and arranged them on her desk to her satisfaction. Jessica was rooting about in the stationery cupboard prior to stocking up the desk drawers, so Nicola left her to it and went into her boss's office to check that everything there was as it should be. She glanced over the large desk and saw that his blotter badly needed renewing, so she removed the soiled layer. As she was slipping in a new sheet she heard a voice wishing Jessica an abrupt 'good morning'; her heart almost stopped beating when she heard the reply, 'Good morning, Mr. Devlin.'

She was still frozen to the spot when the door was thrown open wide, causing a draught which caught the papers on top of the desk and swirled them into the air in every direction. She forgot her nervousness as she darted after them and she had gathered quite a few from the carpet when she turned quickly, still on her knees on the floor, to find that a pair of highly polished shoes had come suddenly into her orbit. She scrambled quickly from her undignified position and felt her cheeks burning with embarrassment as she turned to face him. Annoyed with herself for allowing him to find her in such a predicament, she could hardly bring herself to lift her eyes in his direction.

When she did it was as if she had received a body blow that left her feeling as if the breath had been knocked out of her body. She took one horrified look at him and stepped back filled with disbelief.

'No!' she ejected with stunned dismay. 'No, not you! You *can't* be . . . Matt Devlin!'

He looked down at her from his great height and lifted an inquiring black eyebrow as she continued to stare at him like a mesmerized rabbit. Then he seemed to get an inkling of the reason for her startled recoil. He bent down to peer more closely at her and at the same time he uttered a surprised ejaculation.

'Good lord, it's you!'

Nicola couldn't voice the words she wanted to hurl in his face. The same white-hot fury filled her as it had in the hut when he had so contemptuously kissed her and told her to warn off her friends. Not even in the most horrible of nightmares could an occasion have arisen to match this ghastly situation, and she was wordless in the face of it.

Matt Devlin was the first to recover his composure. A few seconds after his startled recognition of her a twitch showed itself at the corner of his mouth and, though he made an obvious effort to control it, it widened into a grin and then, to Nicola's bitter resentment, he dissolved into helpless laughter.

She watched him vainly try to subdue his amusement till she could stand it no longer and managed with a great effort to find her voice.

'You . . . you monster!' she gasped. 'How dare you laugh at me! I wonder you dare to even look me straight in the eye after your despicable behaviour. You can get yourself another secretary, Mr. Devlin,' she spat out, 'for I wouldn't work for you if you were the last man in the world to offer me employment!'

This remark seemed to get through to him, for he stopped laughing long enough to question her.

'You mean to say you're my new secretary? Good lord!'

The thought seemed to sober him quickly. 'And I thought you were one of the little nuisances who are forever following me about and getting under my feet at every conceivable opportunity! But you must admit,' he chided her, 'that you look a sight different this morning from what you looked yesterday.'

His eyes wandered appreciatively over her with a wicked glint in their depths. 'And you must admit,' he added rather pleadingly, 'that all you girls look alike in those anoraks and trousers that you wear.'

'That,' she answered witheringly, 'does not excuse your behaviour. Nor does it excuse your monumental conceit in thinking every girl who happens to be walking in your vicinity is stalking you with a view to furthering your acquaintance.'

Her sarcasm didn't seem to penetrate his thick skin, for his mouth began to twitch again, but as Nicola watched him suspiciously he made a great effort to keep a straight face as he answered with a slight bow.

'I stand corrected, Miss . . .?'

'Brent,' she bit off.

'Miss Brent . . . And I can only ask you to accept my most sincere apologies for that regrettable episode. I can assure you,' he glinted, 'that if you'll consent to remain in my employment you'll find no fault with my future conduct.' Then changing his slightly mocking tone to one of pleading, he held out his hand and asked her, 'Won't you please change your mind, and stay?'

Nicola knew she was too far committed to clearing Dulcie's name to rebuff his overture, so with a bad grace she grudgingly acknowledged his apology and said primly:

'Very well, Mr. Devlin. I'll stay on that condition.'

He gave a smile of satisfaction as she passed him to go into her own office, for by that time she felt that if she didn't get away from his overpowering presence she would scream.

Once through the door, she leaned thankfully against its panels and expelled her breath slowly, allowing herself a few seconds' grace in which to regain her composure. Mercifully, her office was empty, Jessica's mute curiosity would have been more than she could have borne at that moment, and so she was spared the necessity of pinning on a mask of imperturbability for her benefit. She was furiously angry, with herself as much as with Matt Devlin. She had had no option but to accede to his request to stay, for to leave now would put her out of reach of ever finding out what she wanted to know, what she was determined to know, about her cousin's dismissal. But she hadn't missed the faint glint, quickly masked, that had danced into his dark eyes at her too swift capitulation. He had thought her acquiescence too hurried, as indeed it had been, in the face of her scornful avowal of a moment before that she would never work for him.

Fool! Fool! she berated herself. At least you could have played it cool; as it is now he thinks you're eager to work for him. The conceited devil!

There was a bitter taste in her mouth at this thought and she clenched her fists with impotent fury as she fought the impulse to grab her coat and run as far away from Scaur Bank Mills and their owner as was humanly possible. Before she could do so, however, the door of her office was opened and Jessica sidled in. She quickly brought her angry eyes and mutinous mouth to a semblance of normality before Jessica had time to notice there was anything wrong, and in the ensuing mundane conversation between them she had time to pull herself together and think once more with a cool, calculating mind, the outcome of which was muttered between clenched teeth as the morning progressed and her agitation died down.

You're staying, my girl! However difficult it may turn out to be, *you're staying!*

CHAPTER V

NICOLA had no reason, in the following hours, to regret her decision. Shortly after her interview with her new boss she was summoned to his office by means of the intercom and told to bring her notebook, ready for dictation.

This was the moment she had been dreading. As she gathered up the necessary pad and pencils her hands began to tremble, and when she walked across the small space to his door her knees threatened to give way beneath her as his room took on the aspect of a lion's den.

This wouldn't do at all! She hadn't passed the acid test of their first meeting as boss and employee only to be sent away in disgrace for incompetence in her work. A deep breath and a mighty effort of will sent her into the inner sanctum, and it sustained her until she had reached the chair in front of his desk into which she sank with deceptive grace.

He didn't look up as she entered, his head being bent over a pile of papers with a frown of deep concentration. She waited patiently, wondering a little scornfully if this was a gambit to impress her with his seeming efficiency, and then jumped as his voice cut through her thoughts with cold impersonality.

'Take a letter, Miss Brent . . .' and from that moment she had no time for any other thought but that of the business in hand.

His dictation was swift and concise to the point of abruptness; his command of phrase admirable. Not once did he correct himself or ask her to delete any part of his dictation, and her pencil flew across each line of her notebook as his clear-cut comments were thrust at her with fine disregard for her ability to keep up with him. Nicola's grudging respect changed to exhilaration as her skill was taxed to the utmost and she found he could not defeat her. For the first time since leaving secretarial college she was being called upon to exert herself to the very limit. But a wonderful feeling of satisfaction was her only reward as she transcribed his last sentence. Although he must have known that if a person of less ability had attempted to keep up with him she would have given up in despair, when he finished he didn't even glance up from the paper he was studying as his cold tone dismissed her.

She gathered up her belongings and retreated to her office, feeling a triumphant glow at having passed what she felt had been a deliberately gruelling test of her prowess, and she settled down at her typewriter determining that his letters would be immaculately typed, and delivered in double quick time. If he had any fault to find with her, it would not be within the area of her work, for she was almost certain he would take a wicked delight in pointing out any error, however small, that chanced to halt his raking inspection.

Half-way through her typing, however, the door was opened and he stepped into her room to leave word that he was leaving and wouldn't be returning until later that evening. She acknowledged his message unsmilingly, and he moved towards the door, giving her an inscrutable look as he did so. She willed herself to look away and continued with her typing as if oblivious of his bulk filling the room till it seemed to shrink to miniature. He watched her for a moment longer with eyes that missed nothing of the slender grace of her body as she sat with fierce concentration at her work. A few fleeting rays of sunshine had filtered through the window and were trapped in her red-gold hair. The sight halted his steps as they formed a nimbus of glittering beauty around her bent head, and she missed his involuntary gasp of appreciation, drowned as it was by the clatter of her typewriter, as he watched them glorify the molten beauty of her hair.

Just as suddenly as they had come, the sun's rays disappeared, dispersed by the heavy grey cloud that cloaked them, leaving the room looking momentarily dimmed as if a thousand candles had been extinguished simultaneously, and he quickly averted his eyes as she looked up, surprised to see him still standing there, and sent him a questioning look. To her mystification he seemed at a loss for words and his look was, if it were at all possible to ascribe such an adjective to Matt Devlin, almost sheepish!

She was even more confused when he cleared his throat as if having to make an effort to speak, then he changed his mind and sketched a perfunctory salute before disappearing through the door that led to the corridor outside.

Thoughtfully, she wandered over to the window from where she could look down on to the car park, and was just in time to see him ease his wicked-looking roadster from out of the space reserved for directors' cars and point its nose in the direction of the town. She watched until it was no longer visible, then sat down once more at her desk, her expression marred by a puzzled frown, to continue with her work.

She typed steadily until lunchtime and had almost finished the letters when Edith Stern entered, dressed in her outdoor clothes, to see if she was ready to go to the canteen. Nicola hadn't noticed how the time had flown and when she stopped to consider, realized she was quite hungry. Jessica had gone for her lunch almost an hour before, so she set out some work for her to do when she returned and gladly joined Edith for a meal and an hour's relaxation.

Edith gave her a sympathetic grin as they walked together towards the door.

'Rather overpowering, the Devlins, don't you think?'

Feeling that Edith had the nation's gift of understatement, Nicola nodded her head in agreement, but didn't comment.

Edith chuckled and tucked her arm into Nicola's.

'I know exactly how you feel, my dear. Having worked for one of them myself for the past twenty years I feel qualified to prescribe a good hot meal and half an hour with your feet up to rid you of that "Devlin hangover". After that you'll feel a new woman. Believe me, I've tried it, so I *know*!'

In the days that followed, Nicola was more than thankful to take Edith's advice. It didn't take long for her to discover that the majority of the work of the running of the Mill fell on Matt Devlin's broad shoulders and she was left in no doubt as to his ability to cope. His capacity for work was amazing. He seemed to know intimately the workings of each department and could inform, and command the respect of, each of the departmental heads with whom he was often closeted for hours upon end, discussing, rejecting, and finally resolving whatever crisis had arisen.

His manner remained aloof and businesslike, and Nicola sometimes wondered if she had imagined the circumstances of their first meeting, for he could not have been more circumspect in his behaviour towards her.

Perversely, she felt a little piqued at being treated with such meticulous courtesy and was often tempted to steal a glance from under her lashes when taking dictation, to see if she could surprise a look of softening on his granite-like features, but somehow she had never been able to bring herself to do so; her eyes seemingly unwilling to betray the dictates of her conscience.

Almost without realizing it, Nicola found herself regarding him with unwilling admiration. His uncle did not seem to bother much with the business, for she had yet to meet him. Edith had told her he delegated most of his work to her and if anything came up that needed his immediate attention she would take her car and drive up to the house to discuss it with him.

'He very seldom comes to the works now,' she had told Nicola. 'Ever since Matt took over he's seemed content to potter about the garden or spend his time on his favourite stretch of river, fishing.'

'But isn't that a bit unfair of him,' Nicola had protested, 'to leave his son with all the work?'

Edith had shrugged her shoulders. 'Oh, Matt enjoys work. In fact, he's a demon for it!'

Nicola had inwardly fervently endorsed this statement, having as she did to share his enthusiasm for working under pressure.

Edith and she had formed the habit of lunching together each day and when they finished their meal Edith usually went into town in her car to do a few bits of shopping while Nicola made her way home to take Rufus for a run before going back to work.

She was on her way, after a particularly busy morning, to pick up Rufus, who was generally waiting with his nose through the garden gate for his first glimpse of her, and she smiled as she rounded the corner of the path and heard his excited whimpering. Her aunt was out on one of her many luncheon engagements, so she didn't bother to go into the house. After a swift, damp welcome from Rufus, he rushed past her to take the path to the river, their usual route, and she followed him, drinking in the cool, fresh air that made her gasp a little as the glacial nip of it filled her lungs. Their lunchtime walks were, of necessity, brief, and after ten minutes they made their reluctant way back towards the house. She closed the gate firmly behind Rufus and refused to meet the doggy entreaty in his liquid eyes.

'Later,' she admonished him. 'You know very well this lunchtime walk is a bonus, you scallywag, so you needn't look at me like that!' She felt his eyes on her back until she had rounded the corner and was still smiling as she walked into her office.

Her entry seemed to startle Jessica, whose eyes darted to the inner door expectantly.

'Good afternoon, Jessica. How are you getting on with the work I left you?'

Nicola pretended not to notice that the pile of invoices she had left for Jessica's attention had not appreciably diminished, and smiled at the young girl's guilty squirm as she settled at her desk.

She pointed at the door of Matt Devlin's office and whispered, 'He's got company.'

Nicola raised inquiring eyebrows. 'Is that so unusual?' she frowned.

Jessica grimaced. 'No, but his guest is.' She mouthed silently, 'It's *her* !'

'Her?' echoed Nicola, mystified.

'You know, Aline Royston. She works in Designing. Everyone knows she's after him,' she finished rather vulgarly.

Before Nicola could reprimand her for this uncharacteristically cheeky statement, her phone buzzed, indicating she was required by her boss, and she walked towards the door, slightly prepared by Jessica's information for what lay within.

But nothing could have prepared her for the cosy tableau that confronted her when she entered the office. Her cheeks began to burn as she took in the intimacy of the scene.

Aline Royston was stretched out full length on the black leather settee, one ankle prominently displayed as she negligently twisted and turned her foot, contemplating her flimsy sandal with seeming satisfaction. She was very blonde and very beautiful. Her voluptuous figure was emphasized by the black stretch tights she wore and by the fine cashmere sweater that clung in all the right places. Her full lower lip was pouting at Matt as he looked down at her from where he sat perched on the arm of his chair which he had drawn up near to the settee, and as Nicola entered the room she heard her protest :

'But, Matt darling, you promised to take me to this new roadhouse. You know you did . . . !'

And his negligent answer. 'I haven't forgotten, Aline. But it's out of the question tonight. Perhaps next week . . .'

For some reason Nicola was glaring at him with resentment when he turned towards her and she masked her eyes with an appalled gasp as she realized, by his elevated eyebrows, that she had been too obviously showing her displeasure. She lowered her gaze to the carpet as embarrassment overwhelmed her, and could have died with shame as his voice, that same hateful voice she had heard from him once before in the hut where she had first met him, snaked out and caught her with its lash of sarcasm when he taunted her.

'We must be more circumspect in front of my secretary, Aline. She patently doesn't approve of dalliance during office hours !'

Nicola's humiliation was complete when Aline turned a lazy eye in her direction and didn't trouble to cloak her contempt of secretaries in general, and this one in particular, when she said :

'But, darling, you know how secretaries like to keep the

boss to themselves! I see I'll have to keep a closer watch on you *now*!'

The emphasis was not lost on Nicola, and a sparkle of indignation lit up her green eyes as she opened her lips to inform them both of her true feelings towards her boss. But before she could speak, Matt held up his hand, stilling the words on her lips with a gesture, and turned towards Aline with a grim smile.

'I must ask you to excuse us, Aline. We really have a tremendous amount of work to get through this afternoon. And didn't you say you were busy with a spectacular new design you've dreamed up . . .?'

Aline accepted her dismissal with good grace, so far as Matt was concerned, but turned when she reached the door to send a malevolent look in Nicola's direction, and the barb in her parting remark made Nicola want to forget such things as civilization and lady-like manners and smack her hatefully mocking face.

'All right, Matt dear. But you won't forget the outcome of allowing your last secretary too much rope, will you? After all,' she paused to send a flicker of dislike in Nicola's direction, 'it's every girl's dream to marry her boss . . . a boss such as you, that is!'

The silence in the room could be felt when she closed the door behind her. Nicola's eyes were brilliant with indignation when he turned towards her and it was all she could do to choke out the words.

'What did she mean by that remark about your last secretary?'

He gave an exasperated quirk of his eyebrows and shrugged his shoulders as if disowning completely the capriciousness of women as he answered curtly:

'Don't concern yourself with Miss Royston's remarks, Miss Brent. I certainly don't intend to delve into the illogicality of any speech between two women who have obviously taken an active dislike to each other on sight. The vagaries of women's minds are beyond me, I'm afraid!'

She gasped at this manifestation of glaring injustice. Not one word had she uttered in her own defence even though it had taken every ounce of will-power she possessed not to do so. But this was the very first lead she had had in connection with her cousin and she forgot her own battered feelings for the moment in an attempt to find out more about the derogatory reference to Dulcie.

'I consider Miss Royston's remarks as being beneath contempt,' she countered with icy disdain, 'but I should like to know more about my predecessor's dismissal.'

His black eyebrows drew together in a sharp frown.

'And who, may I ask, informed you that my last secretary had been dismissed?'

Too late, she realized she had slipped up. Her efforts to pump Edith had been met with cool evasion and she had been reluctant to press for information in case of arousing suspicion and perhaps being questioned as to her interest in a girl whom it was supposed she didn't know. She had met with a blank wall, too, when she had put out feelers in Jessica's direction, for she professed to being in complete ignorance of the circumstances of the case, having been in the typing pool at the time and therefore completely out of touch with the directors' offices.

She thought rapidly, but could come up with nothing more convincing than a stuttered, 'Oh, I'm not quite sure who mentioned it. Someone in casual conversation, I think!'

His frown deepened as he stood regarding her thoughtfully. Her cheeks burned as she withstood his gaze. She felt his probing eyes were searching for the truth and she evaded his look lest his penetrating gaze should uncover the guilty shame she felt at her duplicity.

His cold voice smote her ears and her heart gave a lurch of alarm at the words he dropped with glacial rebuff.

'As you seem so very interested in the affairs of my previous secretary, Miss Brent, I shall deem it necessary to inform you that she was dismissed for . . . industrial misconduct, shall we say, for the want of a better term? And now,' with studied sarcasm, 'if your curiosity has been satisfied, perhaps we can get on with some work !'

She met his eyes as the questioning tone jabbed through the sick feeling of dismay his words had effected but managed to hide from him the doubts and uncertainties that were seething in her mind.

Even as she competently took down his dictation and answered his few sharp queries regarding the job in hand the questions nagged at her conscience.   Had Dulcie lied to her mother when she insisted she had been dismissed without reason?   Or, worse still, had her aunt lied to cover up for her daughter?

Nicola thought he would never finish.   Doggedly, she pushed the worrying thoughts from her mind until such time as she could take them out and examine them without distraction.   His voice carried on incisively as he ruthlessly diminished the pile of paperwork on his desk, and she transcribed automatically, her unruffled composure giving lie to the churned-up feelings she was only just managing to hide.

At last she was free to escape to her own office. Jessica looked up from her work and gasped with sympathy as she noted the almost defeated look Nicola didn't bother to hide now that she was safe from Matt Devlin's keen perception, and she immediately jumped up to plug in the electric kettle and gather together the wherewithal to make a pot of tea.

Nicola accepted her cup with a grateful look and

Jessica sat quietly watching her drink as if the tea were sustenance she had long been deprived of.

Tentatively, when Nicola had finished her tea but had, as yet, made no move to start on the pile of work waiting for her, she volunteered:

'I heard what she said, Miss Brent. Please don't let her upset you, for she isn't worth it. As a matter of fact,' she added with glee, 'you must have her worried for her to unsheath her claws like that in front of Mr. Matt. She doesn't welcome competition, from what I've heard!'

Nicola dragged her thoughts back from her aunt and Dulcie as Jessica's remarks sank in. She knew she ought not to encourage the girl's views of her superiors in such a way, but her open-hearted concern was very comforting and she felt she simply couldn't reprimand her, so she smiled and remained silent.

Encouraged, Jessica became bolder. She had developed a bad case of hero-worship in the time she had worked with Nicola, and her blood boiled at the thought of her idol being snubbed by the high-and-mighty Aline Royston who was cordially detested by every girl who came into contact with her.

'Thinks she's the cat's whiskers, she does. And why? Because she doesn't have to work for a living like the rest of us. Oh, no! Her dad's worth as much as the Devlins, if not more! She only works here to satisfy her artistic instinct—she says—but it would be nearer the truth if she were to admit she just comes here to be near Mr. Matt. As if he would look at her when you're around, Miss Brent!'

Nicola felt bound to protest as Jessica's opinions became more forcible and she tried to stem her eloquence before she said anything more. Although she felt bound to agree with everything she said, except her last remark, of course, she had a position of authority to maintain besides an unwilling loyalty to her employer.

'That's enough, Jessica. Miss Royston's affairs are no concern of ours. But even,' she could not resist the oblique dig, 'if what you say is true, then I, for one, am of the opinion that no couple could be better suited.'

Jessica, although rebuked, could not suppress an indignant disclaimer.

'Oh, no, Miss Brent! Why, Mr. Matt is wonderful! And far too good for *her*. All the girls in the main office are mad about him. That's why we started the lottery . . . !'

She gave an appalled gasp and clapped her hand over her mouth. 'Ooh! I shouldn't have mentioned that, Miss Brent. The girls will be mad at me if they find out I've spilled the beans,' she wailed. 'Please promise you won't repeat it?'

Despite herself, Nicola was intrigued. 'What lottery, Jessica?'

'I . . . I can't say any more, Miss Brent. Please don't ask me. It's supposed to be a secret!'

'Does it concern Mr. Matt?'

'Ye . . . es.'

Nicola hadn't the faintest inkling of what might be to come, but she felt bound to probe deeper.

'I think you'd better tell me, Jessica. I promise I won't tell anyone. And besides, I think you should remember you are in a responsible job now, and your loyalty lies with your boss and not with the girls in the typing pool. We're here to protect Mr. Matt from any small annoyances as well as to do the normal office work. Do you understand?' she asked gently.

Jessica's hesitation was momentary. She had obviously never thought of herself as a guardian of her boss's privacy and reacted as Nicola hoped she would. In a tone of slight condemnation, as befitted her newly realized position, she began to explain.

'Well, Miss Brent, it all started with those silly girls in the typing pool having a bet on whether or not it would be possible for a girl to get Mr. Matt interested in her—an ordinary girl, that is—such as a typist like themselves. Some said it couldn't be done as he would be interested only in the more sophisticated type like Aline Royston, for instance. But some of the other girls insisted there were girls in the office who were quite as attractive, if only they could get him to notice them.'

Nicola's lips quirked with amusement at these sentiments, but she suppressed her smile in case the sight of it should halt Jessica's confidences. She needn't have worried, however, for now that she had started Jessica had every intention of finishing the tale and she carried on with engaging frankness.

'That,' she breathed with restrospective enjoyment, 'was when we hit upon the idea of a lottery. I can't remember who first suggested it, I think it might have been Jean Templeton—but anyway it hardly matters as we all thought it a great idea. It was agreed that we would all put two shillings a week into a kitty as prize money and each week we would all put our names in a hat, and the one whose name was pulled out would be the winner for that week!'

'The winner?' Nicola echoed weakly. 'The winner of what?'

'The winner,' Jessica spurted on, 'would be entitled to a clear field for one week only. She'd have one week in which to manage to cultivate an acquaintance with Mr. Matt. Not just to speak to him, such as to say good morning, or anything as banal as that. But to get him to make some sign that she had made a definite impression on him.'

'And that,' Nicola suddenly saw the light, 'is why

Mr. Matt is continually being pestered by young girls every time he sets foot outside his office!'

Here then was the explanation of his seemingly conceited remark about telling her friends to keep their distance! Each week a different girl, egged on by her friends and by the incentive of winning the first prize in the office lottery, was being let loose on the poor unfortunate man, to the detriment of his leisure hours. No wonder he had been angry!

Another remark, puzzling at the time, that had been floating in the back of her mind, was suddenly clarified. His half serious, half cryptic, 'But you must admit that you girls all look alike in those anoraks and trousers you wear.'

She could see them now. The young typists, usually immaculately and fashionably dressed during office hours and when on their way to dances or similar functions, but sensible enough to have learned that mini-skirts don't marry well with the icy winds blowing straight from the snow-covered peaks of the Fells that surrounded them. In their pursuit of Matt Devlin in his free time they would, of necessity, have had to trail him across the rolling hills surrounding the valley in which the Mill nestled and so their apparel would most likely be the favourite brightly-coloured anoraks and stretch pants that were worn, almost uniformly, by the girls as casual outfits.

Nicola's humiliation was a physical pain as she bravely analysed the facts, as he must have seen them, and followed them to their natural conclusion; *his* obvious assessment of their first meeting, which must have been that she had deliberately followed him to scrape up an acquaintance!

Jessica was alarmed at Nicola's pallor—alarmed and puzzled. She knew, of course, that the lottery would be frowned upon by those in authority, but it was, at worst, a harmless prank and hardly warranted the look, almost of horror, that was written on Nicola's face at that moment.

'Are you mad with us, Miss Brent?' she faltered.

Nicola forced a reply from lips dry with anger. Anger, not against the foolish young office girls nor, strangely enough, against Matt Devlin. The anger was directed against herself for allowing herself to be forced into a position where she would have to swallow her pride, subdue the impulse that urged her to pack her bags and run as far away from Scaur Bank Mills as she possibly could, instead of having to don a mask of cool impersonality, as she knew she was committed to do, and face him every day with the knowledge knotted inside her that he was deluding himself he had made yet another conquest!

She couldn't have said what reply she gave to Jessica, but it seemed to satisfy her, for she moved back to her desk to make a start, once again, on the pile of invoices that awaited her attention.

Nicola's energy seemed to have drained away from her. She watched Jessica's nimble fingers rattling away on the keyboard of her typewriter and knew that she, too, should be working on the letters that were lying mocking her from her notebook. All she could think about at that moment was the unpalatable fact that she was classed in Matt Devlin's eyes as a silly predatory female who wouldn't hesitate to throw herself in the way of any man who happened to take her fancy. She was puzzled by one incident in particular—that kiss. What had been his motive in kissing her? Why, if he had thought her to be one of the 'young nuisances', as he had expressed them, and if he had wanted to be rid of them and their annoying presence, he had kissed her? Surely he realized that a kiss to a susceptible teenager was adding fuel to the fire and was certainly not to be classed as a deterrent as he had intimated?

Jessica gave her a startled look as she heard her give a hollow laugh, quite bereft of amusement. She wasn't consoled, either, by the unfathomable look on her idol's face. What her reaction would have been if she could have read Nicola's mind at that moment would be hard to imagine. She had just realized the distasteful fact that she was the unqualified winner of the Devlin lottery!

CHAPTER VI

BY calling upon every ounce of determination she possessed, Nicola finally managed to complete her work in time to pick up her aunt from the house of one of her friends, where she had been having tea and a long leisurely gossip, and reach home before the headache that had started that afternoon finally threatened to overwhelm her.

Her aunt's prattling conversation as they drove home in the little green mini-car Nicola had purchased the previous week was nearly driving her mad, and it was with great relief that she drove the car through the open gates of their home and up the short drive to come to rest at the bottom of the steps that led the way to the front door.

Sarah was so pleased with the new car she could hardly bear to leave it. It had been her sole topic of conversation that afternoon, and indeed every day since it arrived she had managed to buttonhole some unfortunate member of the community who hadn't heard of her good fortune and had proceeded to remedy that omission.

Nicola had borne it all with good-humoured tolerance and a fervent hope that other people would do the same but, today, her aunt's self-satisfied manner had seemed tinged with patronage when she bid farewell to her less fortunate friend and it had begun to jar on her.

The combination of her irritation with her aunt and the throbbing of her temples made her voice sharper than was her wont when she spoke, and Sarah's lip drooped petulantly at her tone.

'Please get a move on, Aunt Sarah! I'm dying for a cup of tea.'

Sarah, who had given no thought to the fact that Nicola had had nothing to eat since lunchtime and had put in a hard day's work besides, looked reproachfully at her and did as she was bid.

'All right, Nicola! There's no need to take that tone. I'm coming!'

Nicola sighed but said nothing. She led the way to the door and when she opened it and walked into the hall she was not surprised to hear her aunt say sulkily:

'I'm going straight to my room, Nicola.' She put a languid hand to her head. 'I think I'm going to have one of my headaches, so I'll leave you to get your own tea. I know you won't mind.'

Without waiting for an answer she turned towards the stairs and began to ascend them, self-pity proclaiming itself from every line of her back, and Nicola watched her go, for once, without compunction.

It seemed too much of an effort to make tea just for herself, so she poured a glass of milk and set it on a tray with a few biscuits, then carried it into the sitting-room where she put it down beside her favourite chair by the window.

Rufus, her constant shadow, settled himself beside her and Nicola sat, her scratch meal untouched, and let the peace of the room seep into her spirit and dull the pulsating nerve at her temples.

Gradually, a little of the tension inside her relaxed and she sat on, her head against the soft back of the chair, deliberately keeping her mind a blank so that the thoughts she knew she would have to sort out were kept at bay.

The awful suspicion that her cousin, perhaps even her aunt, had not told the whole truth when they had said they knew of no reason why Dulcie should have been dismissed had to be faced some time, but just now her mind was a frozen inanimate substance and Nicola was willing it to stay that way, for there were other problems, all bound up with Matt Devlin, that would fast encroach upon her mind if she were to allow herself to think at all.

Just as she was drifting into sleep the telephone rang. Rufus growled softly as Nicola stirred and as it shrilled out once more she groaned and dragged herself from her comfortable position to walk over to answer it.

'Hello?' she queried.

'Nicola? It's me, Liz.'

Immediately, Nicola was alert. Liz's voice was a friendly oasis in the midst of barren isolation and she greeted her with consequent warmth because of it.

'Liz, darling! How are you? How lovely of you to call me!'

Liz's voice when she answered was warm but had an undertone of anxiety.

'Nicola, when are you coming back to London?'

Nicola's heart gave a lurch of foreboding, not so much at the question as the tone of her friend's voice.

'Why? Is something wrong? Tell me quickly, Liz. Has something happened to Dulcie?'

Liz gave a short bitter laugh. 'Nothing's happened to that young woman that hasn't been meant by her to happen. She's perfectly fit, if that's what you mean, Nicola. But I'm at the end of my tether, as far as she's concerned, and if you can't assure me that you'll be back here soon then I'm afraid I'll have to give up the flat and move elsewhere!'

'But, Liz, what's happened?' Nicola broke in anxiously. 'What has Dulcie done to upset you?'

She heard Liz give a sigh and, after a slight pause during which Nicola's overworked imagination ran riot, she began to speak quickly, the words spilling out rapidly as she voiced her indignation.

'I just wish you could see this flat, Nicola! I've just got in after a hard day and Dulcie's obviously been in before me and gone out for the evening. There's a pair of her shoes on this table, right beside the telephone; her clothes are scattered over every bit of the furniture; the cupboard doors are all hanging open, she's even,' Liz's voice seemed to break at the injustice of it all, 'left an overturned bottle of nail varnish on top of our lovely polished occasional table, and Nicola,' she wailed, 'it's running on to the carpet!'

Liz heard Nicola's gasp of horror and it seemed to add fuel to her indignation. 'Yes, and that isn't all! She's taken up with a really wild lot of kids and she brings them back here two or three nights a week, sometimes at midnight. The row they make is dreadful, and the mess . . .! I've no option but to clean it up, for Dulcie makes no effort whatever. So you see, Nicola, why I can't put up with it another day! If there's no chance of you coming back then I'll move in with Jill Harrig. She's looking for a flatmate and I've to let her know by the end of the week, as she has someone else in mind if I don't want to share with her.'

Nicola was horrified. To a person of Liz's temperament the situation she had just described would be sheer misery, and the thought that she had let her friend in for such an existence was unbearable. She tried to find words to apologize for her cousin, but could find none. This, on top of the day she had had, was the final straw and she simply couldn't cope with any more.

'Oh, Liz!' she choked into the mouthpiece. Then she couldn't go on, for tears were threatening to spill from her wide green eyes and her throat was constricted with the hopelessness of it all.

'Nicola!' Liz's voice was high-pitched with amazement. 'You're not *crying*, are you?'

'No . . . of course not!' Nicola's voice wobbled

miserably. But before she could pull herself together and put a semblance of conviction into her tone Liz accused her :

'But you are, Nicola. I can tell! What on earth are they doing to you up there? You never used to cry, whatever happened. Are you unhappy, love?'

The sympathy and genuine feeling in Liz's voice was Nicola's undoing and she began to cry in earnest, softly and hopelessly, the sound carrying straight to Liz's ears and to her heart. Mentally kicking herself for being so full of her own troubles and for pouring them out to her friend without thought of what she might be already having to bear from a selfish aunt and goodness only knew who else, Liz pleaded softly, her own anger forgotten :

'Nicola, love, please don't cry. Nobody's worth all that sorrow. I'm a selfish pig for bothering you with my petty grievances and I want you to forget I ever mentioned them. Will you?'

But Nicola had had time to recover her composure and was shamed by her unaccountable weakness. She tried to explain to Liz that she was just feeling a bit low and that she had nothing at all to worry her, really. And that the sound of her friend's voice had made her give way to a temporary melancholy that was quite uncharacteristic.

Liz listened to her explanation without interruption and made small comforting noises now and again to show she understood. But then she confounded Nicola, at the end of her explanation, by asking mischievously:

'Nicola, pet, have you fallen in love up there in the frozen north?'

'In love . . .?' Nicola's voice was incredulous.

'Yes, in L-O-V-E,' Liz spelled out. 'It happens to all of us, you know. And you sound as if you're going through the first symptoms of an affair that isn't quite working out. Am I right?'

'No! Of course you're not right!' Indignation spilled out over the miles that separated them, and if Nicola could have seen the smile that had lightened Liz's countenance she would have been more indignant than ever. Mercifully, she couldn't, and Liz was careful to keep the smile out of her voice as she answered her.

'All right, all right! I only thought ...'

'Well, you're quite wrong ...!'

'If you say so ...'

'I do say so.' Nicola's voice was rising every minute and Liz thought it was time to end her teasing.

'Well, I'm not sorry to hear it, for if you *were* to fall for someone up there you wouldn't be likely to return to London, would you?'

'I'll be back as soon as I possibly can, Liz, for I can't wait to shake the dust of this place off my feet. Do you think,' unconsciously pleading, 'you could hold on for another week or two if I write to Dulcie and give her a piece of my mind? Truly, I won't be long till I'm back, Liz, and I should hate to have to find another flatmate when I return.'

'Of course I can, darling! I feel better already, having got it off my chest. I can cope with Dulcie and her friends so long as I know you'll be back shortly.'

'Oh, thank you, Liz. I promise I'll be as quick as I can. I just have one problem to clear up, then I'll be on the first train to London.'

They chatted for a few more seconds and then rang off, after arranging a special time suitable to them both when they could speak to each other at least once each week while Nicola was in Carswell.

Although they finished their conversation on most cordial terms, the upsetting interlude had done nothing to help Nicola's headache. A few minutes after Liz's call the pains were once more stabbing at her defenceless head and, early though it was, she decided to take two aspirins and go to bed in the hope that she would sleep it off.

But it was no use. All through the night she tossed and turned as she tried to woo sleep. She tried counting sheep and numerous other dodges she had heard of from time to time, but none of them did the trick. When the heavy blackness of her bedroom began to lighten with the dawn she was still wide awake and physically and mentally exhausted.

Wearily, she dragged her aching limbs from the bed when her alarm sounded. For a while she dallied with the idea of pleading sickness and staying away from work, but then she thought of the questions she would probably be faced with from her aunt, and changed her mind.

After a bath and a cup of tea she felt a little more able to face the office, and Matt Devlin. Cowardice forced her to refuse to think of meeting him with the knowledge she had so recently gained still fresh in her mind, and she reached the Mill in a state of numbed acceptance that the day had to be lived through like any other.

Mercifully, he didn't arrive until after their coffee break, and by then Nicola was able to gather the scattered remnants of courage around her and walk into his office with a steady, if unwilling, tread.

He was sitting at his desk when she went in and looked up sharply when she reached her chair and subsided into it with less than her usual grace.

She kept her gaze on her shorthand pad and so missed the keen glance that raked her face and the look of concern that chased across his dark features.

Abruptly, he pushed back his chair and walked across to the window.

'Come here, Miss Brent.'

'What did you say . . . ?' she asked blankly.

'I said, come over here, Miss Brent.'

His attitude was one of command and he sounded capable of forcing her over to the window if she didn't obey, so, reluctantly, she forced herself to walk towards him.

The glare from the window was as cold and merciless as the dark scrutiny she suffered, with inward withdrawal, from his questing eyes. She struggled to find the courage to meet his look, but her eyes seemed glued to the carpet and would not venture to meet his.

She was dumbfounded, a second later, to feel her chin lifted in firm capable fingers and a voice whose tone she would never have associated with him, asking her gently :

'What troubles you, Miss Brent? What—or should I say who—is responsible for those dark circles beneath your eyes and for that fine-drawn—too fine-drawn—look?'

Surprised, she lifted her downcast lashes and let her green eyes meet his. The sight of the unusual tenderness in their depths threw her into confusion and her first indignant denial stuck in her throat and would not be voiced.

He probed deeper. 'Are you having some trouble with your work? Or at home, perhaps . . . ?'

Fear that he would begin to question her about her home circumstances and so involve her in more distasteful evasion loosened her tongue.

'No . . . ! No! There's nothing wrong, Mr. Devlin, I assure you. I . . .' she improvised quickly, 'I had a restless night last night, that's all. But I feel perfectly well.'

He looked far from satisfied with her explanation and opened his mouth to speak. She steeled herself to more inquisition, but before his words were uttered a child's squeal halted him and they both instinctively looked towards the window and down upon the swathe of green that led to the river.

Nicola's gasp of horror was echoed by Matt Devlin, but as she stood there frozen to immobility he was galvanized into action. He rasped out instructions to her to telephone the surgery for the sister-in-charge as he raced out of the room, divesting himself of his coat as he ran. Nicola couldn't tear herself away from the window and the sight that had so startled them.

Teetering on the edge of the river bank was a child of about three years old. His tiny hands, holding a piece of bread, were extended towards the swans that were gliding gracefully along the surging spate of water rushing along to throw itself over the edge of the dam and into the bay below. It was obvious that he was about to lose his balance, for his little feet were sliding in the clay at the river's edge, but his interest in the swans made him oblivious to danger and he gurgled encouragement to them as he held out the bread enticingly. The scream of fear must have come from an older child who was standing near, as frozen with fright as Nicola herself, gazing with mesmerized eyes at the intent little figure who was within inches of drowning.

Just as they knew it would, it happened! The child's attention was distracted for a minute and a sudden movement of his body overbalanced him into the water. The older child gave another terrified scream that faded to a choke as a figure darted past him and dived, straight as an arrow, to the spot where the little one had disappeared.

Nicola shook off the paralysing fear that held her as she saw Matt Devlin hit the water. With trembling haste she dialled the surgery and informed the sister of the drama being enacted beneath their very windows. When the sister assured her she was almost on her way, she ran out of the office and down to the river, swollen by melted snow from the hills, to give what help she could.

All the way down the stairs she was praying, 'Please, God, let him be safe! Please, God, let them *both* be all right!'

Fear lent wings to her feet and she dashed away the tears that were blinding her as she ran to the spot where she had last seen them.

An appalled tremor shook her when she reached the spot and could see nothing. No black head showed itself above the brackish, cream-frothed water, no child's scream of horror pierced the almost deafening din as thousands of tons of water fell, just a few yards downstream, into the deep bay below.

Just then, as her eyes were drawn in the direction of the edge of the fall, she saw them! Matt Devlin, with the still, quiet figure of the boy in tow, was battling with superhuman strength against the vicious current, and seemed to be winning. Slowly, inch by inch, he was fighting his way back from the edge of the waterfall to try to get into calmer waters. Nicola's heart swelled with anxiety as she watched him, his face grim with effort, hampered by the sodden clothing that was dragging him down and by the bitter cold of the water. She could stand it no longer. She whipped off her shoes and the jacket of her suit and prepared herself to dive in to assist him. But before she took off from the bank, a man's voice shouted almost in her ear :

'No, miss, don't! We've brought a rope. We'll soon have them out!'

Thankfully, she turned and saw a party of men from the Mill, with the nursing sister bringing up the rear, racing along the bank to go to Matt's assistance. In a matter of minutes they had thrown him a rope and a life-belt and were towing him and his burden towards the side.

Willing hands took the boy and delivered him to the nurse, who immediately began to give him the 'kiss of life'. Matt Devlin shook off the hands that would have supported him and dropped to his knees beside them to wait for the first sign of life from the unconscious little form. They were rewarded a few minutes later by a small movement that proclaimed that life was not extinct, and then the hysterical clanging of an ambulance bell impinged upon their consciences. It drew up with a squeal of brakes and they stood back to allow the nurse to enter it with the softly moaning child.

Nicola, meanwhile, had been pushed to the back of the crowd of eager helpers and when she heard the bell that presaged the coming of the ambulance she turned to pick up her coat and shoes from where they lay on the river bank and put them on in an effort to stop the shivering that attacked her limbs as reaction set in.

She desperately wanted to assure herself that he was all right, but now that the drama was almost over, she couldn't bring herself to push through the crowd that surrounded him, so she walked with a slightly wobbly gait back to the office.

She had just reached it, and collapsed into a chair, when he followed after her. She jumped up in dismay as she took in his saturated clothing and the dripping wet hair that was twisted into black curls as the water freed it from its usually scrupulously-groomed state. He stood in the middle of the office and looked down ruefully at the pools of water that were forming round his feet.

Looking up with a quick grin, he was about to speak, but stopped with a sharp-drawn breath when he saw Nicola's face that still mirrored the dreadful anxiety of the last few minutes. He took a step forward, his hands outstretched in involuntary compassion. but he spoke sharply.

'Nicola, don't look like that! It's over now and the little blighter is quite safe.'

She was quite unconscious that he had used her first name. A wave of such feeling swept over her that all antagonism fled and she looked at him with eyes swimming with relief as she choked out:

'Oh, Matt, you were wonderful! That baby . . .! He would have drowned if you hadn't been so quick. And that dreadful moment when I thought you were both being swept over the dam . . .' She gave a shudder as she relived the moment she had first caught sight of them struggling against the force of the waters, only inches from the top of the waterfall, and closed her eyes as if to shut out the terror of it.

She felt his arms grip her shoulders with a leashed strength and wondered at the slight breathlessness in his voice when he queried, 'You were worried about *me*, Nicola?'

Her heart gave a jerk as the question was breathed against her ear and when, at last, she met his eyes, it was as if the world stood still waiting for her answer. She found it difficult to speak against the tumult of emotion that his nearness aroused in her and merely gazed deeply into the fathomless darkness of his eyes. She felt she could have drowned in their black depths. Not the frightened drowning of a panic-stricken soul fighting for his life, but the thankful relinquishing of a quiescent heart into the keeping of its mate.

Her look was answer enough. With a low, triumphant laugh he tightened the arms that held her and bent his head to claim her lips.

That laugh was like a douche of cold water to Nicola. To her distraite ears it sounded exultant; the cry of the conquering male sure of his victory and of the willing submission of his prey.

She jerked away from his embrace with a repugnance

that astonished him. How could she have been so overcome as to allow the man she detested above all others
to think her easy game? She lashed herself inwardly for
allowing her emotions to sink her pride so far as to let
him think the alarm and tension of an upsetting interlude
could possibly justify these last few moments. She had
amused him with her sickening emotionalism, and his
amusement was justified!

Ice tinkled in her voice and self-abnegation gave a
hard glitter to her emerald eyes as she taxed him.

'You forget yourself, Mr. Devlin! Or do your
promises mean nothing? If you remember, I consented
to remain in your employment only on condition that
there would be no repetition of your behaviour at our
first meeting!'

Green eyes challenged black—and black won! As the
colour seeped into her cheeks she turned away in confusion from his eyes that had changed instantly from a
melting smoulder to chips of ebony when she flung her
words at him.

She braced herself to receive the contemptuous whip
of his anger, then slumped against the desk with relief as
he managed to control the violence so visible within him.
With icy disdain, not one whit lessened by the sodden
state of his attire, he bit out hatefully :

'Thank you for reminding me, Miss Brent. I must try
to remember you're too good a secretary to waste on idle
dalliance. It would be ideal, of course, if you were not
so averse to it, but,' with a negligent shrug, 'one can easily
find a sociable companion who has no need of other
qualifications! From now on, Miss Brent,' he said to a
seething Nicola, 'you will have no need to worry. Anything between us will be strictly business!'

CHAPTER VII

THE next morning, as Jessica and Nicola busied themselves with the routine work that preceded Matt Devlin's arrival, they were surprised by the appearance of Miss Sendall.

She was flushed with exertion as she rushed into their office, her spectacles slithering down the bridge of her nose giving her the look of an anxious owl, as she peered over the top of them. They sensed her agitation even before the words spilled from her.

'Oh, Miss Brent! I've just had word from the house. Mr Matt is ill! They've sent for the doctor and they'll let us know later what he says!'

She sat down on the nearest chair in a state of collapse, and Nicola wasn't surprised to see tears welling from her pale, weak-looking eyes.

'The poor dear boy . . .' she went on. 'I knew last night when I saw him rushing to his car in those soaking wet clothes he would suffer for his good deed. He looked dreadful, Miss Brent! So white and tense . . . And he drove away as if a handful of devils were after him. Yes, he looked really upset!' Her quavering voice faded and was lost as she contemplated the scene she had witnessed the previous day, so she missed the flush of guilt that flooded Nicola's face before it faded, leaving her paper-white.

'Is . . .' Nicola cleared the huskiness from a throat tight with misery and tried again. 'Is it serious, do you think?'

Miss Sendall came back to earth with a jerk to answer Nicola with a worried sigh. 'I don't know any more than I've told you, my dear. But I sincerely hope not . . . I do hope not!'

She made her way to the door and wandered into the passage outside, shaking her head with worry as she went.

Jessica gave voice to her feelings as soon as the door closed behind her. She, too, had a look of shock at the news they had been given and she startled Nicola by putting into words the thought she had been thinking.

'I can't imagine Mr. Matt being ill, can you, Miss Brent? He's always so full of life, so energetic! I can't ever remember hearing of his being ill before.' Then she echoed Miss Sendall's sentiments and Nicola's silent plea. 'Oh, I do hope it's nothing serious!'

Nicola's heart gave a throb of pain. All the previous night she had tried to blot his image, his dark compelling looks, out of her mind. She was nothing if not honest with herself, and had faced squarely the knowledge that she was strongly attracted to him. It had appalled her, at first. Liz's voice had reverberated through her mind. 'Are you in L-O-V-E, Nicola?'

Her whole being had rejected the thought. How could she love the son of the man who had been responsible for the death of her parents? It wasn't possible. It *couldn't* be love. Love to her meant mutual respect, the coming of two hearts together with wondering recognition and boundless joy. She had waited all her life for that to happen to her, scorning the endless flirtations of her friends, harmless as they were, in order to save herself for the one person she knew she would meet some day. She had searched her mind, picked up her parents' photograph from her bedside table and stared long and deeply at the treasured item, willing back the feeling of revenge that had started her on her campaign against the Devlins. But all she saw, as she looked into the silver-framed photograph, was Matt Devlin's dark, saturnine features, and she had acknowledged then that, although it could never be termed love, he had a devastating, magnetic attraction for her. The crescendo of feeling that had engulfed her as she watched his struggle against almost insuperable odds had weakened the barriers between them, and the feel of his arms around her and his voice whispering in her ear had swept them away as surely as the mighty force of the river carries everything in its path. Everything, that is, except Matt Devlin. Yesterday it had been cheated of its prey, and for that she was profoundly grateful. Even with the echo of his mocking, triumphant laugh ringing in her ears and the bitter taste of humiliation sour in her mouth, she could still give thanks for that, and for the small crumb of comfort she felt from the thought that he would never know how near she had been to surrendering herself to him completely and without reservation.

She hated herself for her weakness and tried to whip up her scorn of him, fully conscious that the only weapon she had left was pride, and that she must make full use of it to enable her to generate antagonism towards him, as a screen between herself and the purely physical attraction he held for her. . . .

All over the Mill there was whispered conjecture that day. Every face wore a worried frown and the question on everyone's lips was the same, 'Have you heard how he is?'

Nicola worked away in a daze of misery, her mind alert for the phone call that would tell her her worst fears would not be realized. She had sent Jessica for her lunch but had decided to have hers in her office, near at hand in case the phone should ring.

The news, when it arrived, was brought by Edith Stern who had been up at the house all morning, and it was good.

She walked in on Nicola, who was typing away furiously at work for which there was no particular urgency, in order to keep her mind occupied away from thoughts of a Matt Devlin laid low by pneumonia or pleurisy or rambling through the throes of a high temperature, or worse. She sprung up from her desk at Edith's entrance and questioned her with mute appeal, the words she wanted to utter sticking in her throat.

Edith answered her unspoken question hastily, not without small wonder at the amount of regard Nicola's expressive face betrayed to her sympathetic eyes, and was rewarded by a lightening of the shadows on her friend's unhappy countenance.

'It isn't serious, Nicola! In fact, Matt is just about driving everyone frantic up there at the house. When he tried to get up this morning he was dizzy and weak and a bit light in the head. He has the mother and father of colds, poor dear, and small wonder when you consider the soaking he got yesterday and the unaccountable delay in his getting home to a hot bath and a change of clothing. However, when Mrs. Cherry, their housekeeper, saw the state he was in this morning she absolutely refused to allow him to come to the Mill and sent for the doctor. Matt, I believe, was furious with her and there was a battle royal between them until his father walked in to throw his weight on Mrs. Cherry's side. They managed to persuade Matt to be sensible and get back into bed until the doctor arrived. When I got there the doctor was just leaving, and he gave Mrs. Cherry strict instructions that he was to stay in bed for at least another couple of days. He's calling back tomorrow to see how he is. Poor Mrs. Cherry!' Edith said with feeling. 'She'll have a dreadful time with him, for he loathes being laid up. But she'll manage him if anyone can!'

A faint smile touched the corner of Nicola's tremulous mouth as she pictured the scene Edith had just described. She could well imagine Matt being a bad patient, for he was impatient of anything that stayed his tremendous drive and vigour. She sympathized heartily with his housekeeper, Mrs. Cherry.

Edith was well satisfied with the beginning of a smile she saw and wondered, once again, at the scarcely veiled emotion Nicola had shown at her news. The poor child has fallen for him, she thought, and sighed as the vision of loveliness that was Aline Royston floated in her mind's eye. Not much chance of *that* female leech allowing Nicola to appropriate her chosen consort! What she had, she held, and in no uncertain manner. But still, Edith pondered, she's done all the running, up till now. And no one ever knows what goes on in Matt's mind until he's ready to tell them.

Nicola broke in on her thoughts, this time her voice completely under control.

'Do you think I should answer what mail I can until he returns to work, Edith? Or might it be better just to shelve the lot until he's well enough to cope with it himself?'

Edith didn't hesitate. 'Oh, leave it, Nicola. I can say, without fear of correction, that Matt will not thank you for taking over his province, even in such a small matter. If it were his father, now, I could safely say he would welcome having the work taken off his hands. But Matt is another kettle of fish. He likes to have his hand on the helm at all times. And after all,' she went on, 'it'll only be a few days, a week at the most, before he's back at work.'

Edith's decree proved to be the right one, for an hour later Nicola's phone rang. When she answered it she was surprised to hear a man's voice, a voice she did not recognize, asking for her by name.

'This is Miss Brent speaking,' she answered him.

'Oh, good. Charles Devlin here, Miss Brent.'

Her gasp of surprise must have been audible to him, for there was amusement in his tone as he went on.

'I'm calling you on behalf of my son, Matt. I suppose you know he's ... mm ... indisposed, at the moment?'

'Why, yes,' she stammered. 'But I'm so pleased to have heard from Edith ... Miss Stern ... that he's not seriously ill.'

'Hmm ... well, seriously ill or not, he's making enough fuss about being kept in bed. Cherry and I'll finish up being the patients by the time he's on his feet again !'

Although the words were spoken in a mock-stern manner, Nicola could hear the undertone of amusement and deep affection that belied his words, and a laugh crept into her voice when she answered him, forgetting for the moment that the disembodied voice at the other end of the phone was her arch-enemy.

'I'm sure you'll be able to quieten him, Mr. Charles.'

'My dear, I've no intention of trying. That's why I'm phoning you ! The wretched boy insists he won't stay in bed another minute unless I arrange for someone from the office to come here tomorrow with his mail, to take dictation. It's strictly against doctor's orders, you understand, but I've been bludgeoned into agreeing. So will you bring your notebook, and the mail, round here tomorrow about ten? I'll send my chauffeur to pick you up, so you needn't worry about transport, my dear.'

Somehow, Nicola managed to convey, through stiff lips, her agreement to the plan, and he rang off with a grunt of satisfaction.

She walked over to the window and looked out over the rolling meadows in the direction of her beloved hills, as if to find consolation in their majestic beauty. But there was no solace to be found there, for the hills were shrouded by thick grey cloud; the trees on the river banks bent and still under a blanket of drab mist. She turned away from the depressing sight and slumped down in the chair at her desk. Even through the feeling of thankfulness she felt at Edith's cheering dictum on Matt's condition, she had been conscious of a great relief at not having to face him for at least a day or two. But now, with his father's words still ringing in her ears, the emotional turmoil that had settled down to a pulsating throb was churning again inside her. Tomorrow morning! How could she face him, her poise scattered to the winds and with not even the bolstering support of contempt and dislike to help her through the hours she must spend with him. She drooped with dejection as she pondered on the distasteful task before her. Could she run away—now, before the ties that bound her to her job could be impinged upon her conscience? But no! She rejected the thought almost before it was formed. She had pledged herself to clear Dulcie's name, she thought dully, and she owed it to her aunt to stay until she had done so.

Jessica's quick footsteps sounded in the corridor outside. Hastily, Nicola pulled some work towards her and tried to concentrate on the paper in front of her. Jessica's sharp eyes saw too much, at times, and discretion was not her strong point. Nicola was able to turn a composed face towards her when she opened the office door and burst in like a clumsy colt.

'Have you heard, Miss Brent?' she asked with eager concern.

'Yes, I've heard, Jessica. He's not as bad as we thought, and will be back at work in a couple of days. Tomorrow I'm going up to the house with the mail, so I'll leave you in charge of the office while I'm away. I shouldn't be more than a few hours and there's plenty of work to be getting on with.'

'Oh, yes, Miss Brent,' Jessica answered with confidence. 'I'll manage fine. Don't you worry about a thing!'

They settled down to work and for the following hour conversation was desultory. Matt Devlin's drive supplied them with more than enough work each day, and now there was a lull they seized the opportunity of clearing up the backlog of routine work that had been put to one side until they had a chance to get on with it.

At three o'clock Jessica decided it was time for a break and left her desk to switch on the electric kettle and make a cup of tea. Nicola leaned back in her chair for an idle few minutes and watched her reaching up to the top of a cupboard to get a fresh packet of tea. She couldn't quite manage it, so she got the small steps they used for just such an occasion and tripped up them lightly. She twisted round, tea in hand, to make the return journey, but stopped in her tracks when Nicola asked her involuntarily :

'Do you ever think of becoming a model, Jessica?'

She flushed to the roots of her hair and looked at Nicola as if she were a pet dog that had suddenly turned and bit her.

Mortified, she answered sullenly, 'Of course not, Miss Brent.' Then in a rush, 'Are you making fun of me?'

Nicola saw the hurt in her eyes and was puzzled by it. Mystification in her voice, she answered :

'Why on earth should you think I'm making fun of you, Jessica? Nothing is further from my thoughts!'

She knew Jessica was a self-conscious girl, full of inhibitions, and she had been as prickly as a porcupine for the first few days of their acquaintance, but lately she had seemed to shed her sullenness and had begun to treat

Nicola as a friend, especially since the day she had explained about the lottery. She had even told her a little —not much, but enough for Nicola to form a fairly clear picture—about her home life and her family. So, dismayed by her obvious hurt as well as puzzled by it, Nicola pressed her:

'Why do you think such a thing, Jessica?'

She retreated down the steps and stood before Nicola with a glowering look spoiling the youthful contours of her face.

'You know very well,' she scuffed the carpet with her shoe, 'that all the girls make fun of me because I'm ugly and clumsy. And yet . . .' Nicola sensed rather than heard the tears in her voice, 'yet you ask me if I ever think of being a model!'

Nicola gave a gasp of indignation allied with dismay that the child could think her heartless enough to poke fun at her. She wanted to put her arms round her hunched shoulders and assure her that she was every bit as pretty as any of her colleagues, but she knew that would be a mistake. Instead, with her fingers crossed for luck, she decided upon tougher tactics. In a no-nonsense voice she berated her:

'I've never heard anything more ridiculous. Ugly, indeed! Do you realize that often, in the flesh, the photographic model is really not much to look at? The perfect model girl doesn't exist. Every top model is "perfect", but for a different reason. She may be plain but have beautiful limbs. You, Jessica, are what photographers are always on the look-out for. You're *different!* If you look around you you'll see what I mean. Nearly all the girls of your age are so very much alike, as if they'd all been cast in the same mould, but you have an elusive "something" that the photographers would simply itch to work with. Not,' she hastened to add, 'that it would start off a life of tiaras and model gowns. You would first have to enrol at a modelling school for training, and when I say *training* I mean really hard slogging! If you're determined, however, and you make the grade, then the prizes are really glittering.'

Jessica's eyes were like saucers when she finished. All animosity had gone and in its place was the dawning of a wonderful dream. Nicola felt no shame in arousing that dream. The background Jessica had sketched of her home life was appalling. A terraced house full of brothers and sisters in 'steps and stairs'; a bullying, often drunken father; and a mother who accepted as normal the intermittent hidings she received when he staggered home 'in his cups' on a Saturday night. She felt no compunction whatever in letting the girl glimpse another side of life, as different from her own as anything could be, as an incentive to her to climb out of the dismal environment she could well stay in for the rest of her life unless pushed from behind to achieve something better.

Jessica stuttered in her eagerness. 'Do you mean you think I've a chance of becoming a model, Miss Brent? Really and truly think so?'

'I wouldn't have raised your hopes by discussing it, otherwise, Jessica. Would you like me to get in touch with my friend who runs a modelling school to get you more details?'

Jessica's indrawn breath was answer enough without her fervent, 'Oh, *would you*? Oh, thank you, Miss Brent! Thank you!'

Nicola waved away her thanks and told her:

'I expect to be going back to London shortly. Naturally, I'll be going back to the agency, so I'll contact you from there. Meanwhile, take care of your complexion and your figure. No scars or unsightly marks, mind, for that'll put paid to your career as a model.'

To her surprise, Jessica did not show the delight she

had expected. Instead, her jaw dropped with almost comical dismay at her words.

'You're leaving us? But why? I thought you liked it here, Miss Brent. No one said you were only temporary, I understood that you were staying for good.'

Nicola mentally kicked herself for her slip of the tongue.

'I'm sorry, Jessica, I shouldn't have told you that. Will you promise to keep it to yourself? Please? I can't explain at the moment, but, believe me, it's very necessary that I return to London in the near future. As soon as I've cleared up my business in Carswell, in fact. But I wouldn't like it to get around that I'll be leaving, just yet. Can I rely upon you to be discreet?'

Instead of replying, Jessica just nodded absently, lost in thought, and to Nicola's surprise seemed to be in a quandary.

'Jessica?' she asked sharply, waiting for her spoken assurance. She still didn't answer; her brow wrinkled with worry.

Finally she seemed to reach a conclusion, for she looked at Nicola apologetically and coloured guiltily as she asked her:

'Can I tell someone if I swear them to secrecy, Miss Brent?'

'Certainly not, Jessica. I ask you for complete secrecy. No one but we two must know that I'm contemplating leaving the Mill. In any case,' surprise heightened her voice, 'who else would be interested?'

Jessica mumbled something about the girls in the typing pool.

'The typing pool?' Nicola was amazed. 'Why should those girls be interested in what I do?'

Jessica gulped and swallowed hard before dropping her bombshell.

'You remember,' she felt her way with extreme caution, 'what I told you about the lottery?'

'Yes,' Nicola's voice was dry.

'Well, I talked it over with the girls and we decided that it was all rather childish, anyway. And that we didn't really have a chance of getting to know Mr. Matt well enough for him to ask any one of us out. I don't think'—she added restrospectively—'we would have had the nerve to go anyway, so we dropped the idea altogether.'

Nicola breathed a sigh of relief. 'I think you were all very wise,' she smiled.

'Yes, but that left us with the problem of what to do with the money in the kitty . . .' Jessica continued even more slowly.

'And what did you decide?'

Jessica seemed almost to give up the ghost. There was a minute's complete silence while Nicola waited for her to find the words she was so obviously groping for. Then they came out with a rush of reckless abandon.

'We decided to nominate two candidates most likely to attract Mr. Matt, and the ones who voted for the girl who gets him will share the money. One of the candidates is Aline Royston . . .'

'Oh, you girls,' Nicola half-smiled, 'what *will* you get up to next? But I still don't see what all this has to do with my leaving, Jessica?'

'It's just that . . .' Jessica struggled on, 'if you leave, it'll be unfair on the best part of the girls, because most of them have voted for you. You see . . . you're the other candidate!'

Astonishment, dismay, humiliation—Nicola ran the gamut of emotions before searing anger took her by the throat and stayed the tide of mortification that flooded her cheeks. Jessica looked on, rigid with dismay, when she saw the effect her words had had on Nicola. She took a step backward, her hand groping behind her for the handle of the door and, when she found it, she opened it and fled.

What have I done? she wondered fearfully, as she ran to the sanctuary of the cloakroom. One thing was certain. She had no intention of facing her superior until that awful tide of anger had receded. She had looked ready to kill her!

CHAPTER VIII

THE impact of Jessica's announcement had the effect, when her temper cooled and rational thought had taken over, of hardening Nicola's senses and encasing her in a cocoon of self-imposed indifference.

The shock of knowing that the majority of the office staff were convinced that she had designs on Matt Devlin, combined with the knowledge that he also thought her susceptible to his charms, made her shrink into a hard shell of aloof nonchalance that was to fool everybody but herself and perhaps Edith Stern, who was, in any case, the soul of tact and the least likely to gossip or speculate —at least verbally—about the state of her friend's feelings.

Consequently, when she went down to breakfast the next morning she was wearing her new-found courage like a banner, boosted by the awareness of having donned her most becoming outfit. Her aunt unknowingly aided her by expressing the fact that she had never seen her looking prettier—great praise from a woman who seldom noticed and very rarely remarked upon anything not concerning herself or her affairs.

Nicola replied with a bright smile that she was feeling on top of the world, and her aunt, slightly taken aback by this show of early morning exuberance, was completely deceived. As she represented the first hurdle to be conquered in her vendetta against the prying eyes of her associates, Nicola was cheered.

She sat down to her breakfast. It was all going to be so easy, she told herself. All she had to remember was never to let her mask slip, or to allow herself to think as a silly romantic girl might when she came up against Matt Devlin's annihilating appeal. It will be quite simple really, she was thinking, as she gave a valiant impression of eating a hearty meal while every bite was lodging against a lump in her throat as big as an egg, no one will try to pry if I ignore everything that has been said and pretend that I'm completely indifferent. The gossip will soon die down when something more dramatic happens to capture their interest. Meanwhile, it's me against them!

She finished her breakfast and gave her aunt a hasty peck before leaving for the office. She forced her reluctant feet to carry her nearer, but when she reached the door her knees were shaking like a jelly.

Jessica was already seated at her desk and Nicola braced herself for the second test of the day.

'Good morning, Jessica!' she fired her first shot with a pleasant smile and a casual wave in the startled girl's direction.

'Go ... od morning, Miss Brent!'

Jessica's heartfelt sigh of relief could almost be heard as she echoed Nicola's greeting. What she had expected Nicola's attitude to be she could not have said, but her senior's pleasant smile and cheerful countenance was a very welcome sight after the sleepless night she had put in worrying as to whether she would be banished to the typing pool for her impudence of the previous day. For the next hour she fussed around Nicola like an attentive puppy waiting for the pat that would tell her that all was forgiven; but the pat never came.

She was pleasant enough, Jessica pondered, and she was as thoughtful and attentive as ever, but something was missing. She had changed in some indefinable way that was hard to put a finger on, but it was there; a coolness, a vague detachment that teased Jessica with its sheer intangibility. She looked over covertly to where she sat, busy with the morning mail. The cream-coloured suit she was wearing fitted her beautifully, the blouse of pale-green nylon she wore with it giving a trans-lucent brilliance to her eyes and the neutral tone of the suit highlighting the copper tones of her hair. She's like an ice-maiden, Jessica thought, withdrawn and isolated from us ordinary mortals! But I wish she were back to normal. I don't like it. She's friendly but too aloof; I don't think I'll ever be allowed to get really near to her again, our friendship's been spoiled completely!

At ten o'clock prompt, the car arrived to take her to the Devlin house. With calm detachment, Nicola gathered together everything she would need and walked, with head held high, down the stairs to the chauffeur who was waiting beside a light grey Rolls of breathtaking opulence.

She still had feeling enough left to experience a thrill of pleasure at the sheer luxury of the ride. The house was on the outskirts of the town and stood in its own grounds, surrounded by woodland and with velvet-smooth lawns flanking the long drive that led to a carved oak door of magnificent proportions. The chauffeur handed her out of the car, then pulled an ornate antique bell, no doubt to summon someone from the nether reaches of the house. In a matter of minutes, the door was opened by a small buxom woman with a beaming smile of welcome on her round, open face.

'Come away in, my dear,' she beckoned Nicola, 'Master Matthew is waiting for you.'

In a surprisingly cool voice, free of tremor, Nicola re-turned her greeting and asked, 'Young Mr. Devlin is better, then?'

The housekeeper, Mrs. Cherry, pulled a face of in-dulgent resignation as she ushered Nicola into the hall and indicated that she would take her coat.

'That one! He's made my life a misery this last

twenty-four hours with his eternal hankering to be up out
of his bed. I daren't think what the doctor will say
when he finds out about you coming to work with him.
But then,' she shrugged resignedly, 'he knows him almost
as well as I do, so he'll probably expect something of the
sort. There's no holding Master Matthew when he's got
the bit between his teeth, and I must admit that he's very
much better this morning. Come upstairs, my dear, and
see for yourself.'

A nerve twitched slightly at the corner of Nicola's
mouth as she faced the ordeal of a meeting in the confines of his bedroom. She had imagined he would be up
and dressed, waiting to work in one of the downstairs
rooms, but she hesitated only momentarily before following Mrs. Cherry up the stairs. Her eyes took in with
aesthetic pleasure the mellow carved woodwork of the
magnificent staircase which had a pattern of fleur-de-lis
surmounted by a Tudor rose and a mitre. Mrs. Cherry
turned and smiled when she saw Nicola's interest in the
carving. She told her with a hint of pride:

'That's the mitre of Bishop Blaise, my dear, the patron
saint of wool-combers. Master Charles's father was
tickled pink when he bought this house and found out
what that carving represented, said nothing could be
more appropriate for the house of a textile family. He
even called the house Blaise House !'

Encouraged by Nicola's interest, Mrs. Cherry proceeded to point out more of the family treasures as they
progressed towards Matt Devlin's room. Nicola,
although genuinely fascinated by the fine examples of
what were obviously collectors' pieces, was not averse to
the delay, and dallied over the rare Beauvais eighteenth-
century tapestry chair that stood in all its glory in an
alcove just off the corridor along which they were walking. Mrs. Cherry was pleased when Nicola remarked

upon the perceptible care that was taken of the house and its contents.

'I do my best,' she beamed, 'but it's nice to be appreciated, my dear. The men,' she said, 'don't seem to see anything I do, as far as housework's concerned, that is. They're very appreciative of what goes on the table, though, I must admit. But they wouldn't see a bit of dust if they fell over it! Not that there's ever any for them to see,' she bridled, 'I'd soon make my presence felt if there were. But I sometimes wish there was a mistress in the house that I could discuss things with ... It's all very well having things all my own way, but what's the use of that if there's only me to recognize the effort that's been put into things? Yes,' she affirmed once more, 'I'll be more than pleased to see Master Matthew married and bringing a mistress into the house!'

'How long is it since Mr. Matt's mother died?' Nicola asked sympathetically.

'Oh, it must be about twenty years or more. His father too.'

Nicola's forehead wrinkled. 'His father?' she asked, puzzled. 'But Mr. Charles ...?'

Mrs. Cherry looked surprised. 'Don't you know that Mr. Matt is his adopted son? His brother's child?'

At Nicola's obvious perplexity, she explained:

'Mr. Charles's younger brother was a flier. His plane went missing for two days and his poor wife, who was expecting a child at the time, was frantic. It was a dreadful time for all of us. Master Matthew was away at school, fortunately, so he was spared the sight of his mother at her wits' end with worry and his Uncle Charles not fit to speak to for days. He phoned, he wrote, he moved heaven and earth to find out what had happened to his brother, but as luck would have it, he was out when the telegram came to say that wreckage had been found and there was no hope of survivors. Master Matthew's mother was in the hall when the telegram was delivered to the house and no one could prevent her from reading it. It was the death of the poor dear lady; she never recovered from the shock. A few days later she gave birth to a stillborn child and she followed it a few hours later.'

Mrs. Cherry wiped a tear from her eyes as she relived the tragedy, and Nicola was hard put to stay her own tears as she pictured a young lad's bewilderment at being deprived of both his parents in such a short space of time. Nicola felt a rapport with him. They had both lived through the same harrowing experience, had both been left feeling rudderless and without purpose; empty of feeling after the initial blow had fallen.

But all sympathy fled when she remembered her own parents and the part Charles Devlin had played in their death. She listened without interrupting as Mrs. Cherry, in full flood now, went on to tell of how Mr. Charles had adopted Matt and brought him up as his own son, even though he had no wife of his own, and was never likely to have. This last remark puzzled Nicola.

'Why was Mr. Charles never likely to marry?'

'Why? Because the only woman he had ever wanted married someone else, that's why! And I don't think he recovered from the blow!'

All at once, Mrs. Cherry seemed to think she was being too garrulous. She closed her lips as if to swallow the words she was about to utter and turned briskly to Nicola.

'There now, I have run on, haven't I?' She seemed surprised at herself. 'I don't usually chatter on so, my dear. You must be thinking me a proper old gossip, but it's just that it's such a change to have a nice young lady like yourself to talk to. I hope you won't think I make a habit of talking my head off about the family?'

She smiled her relief when Nicola assured her she

thought no such thing, and led the way, without more ado, to Matt Devlin's room.

It was just along the corridor; their feet made no sound as they trod the heavy-piled carpet that led to his door. Mrs. Cherry tapped on the panel and waited until a voice bade her enter. She opened the door, then stood aside for Nicola to precede her.

Her palms moist, Nicola stepped over the threshold. She expelled a slow breath of relief as she entered and saw that it was not, as she had suspected, his bedroom, but a sitting-room, clearly part of a suite, furnished in an aggressively male manner without a trinket or flower of any kind to break the severity of the décor. Stark white emulsioned walls; two settees covered in golden tobacco-brown velvet and a pony skin rug on the floor repeating the colour; a low dark-wood table with two large glass ashtrays; nondescript green curtains of soft velvet that had been pushed aside without regard for any kind of symmetry, just a seeming impatience for more light to fall upon the large desk that must surely have grown there beneath the immense windows.

Matt Devlin rose from the desk as Nicola walked into the room. She faced him with a bravado she did not feel, and was dismayed at his pallor. He was wearing a dark blue dressing-gown that accentuated his paleness and made his dark eyes seem an incredible black. He stood silent, deliberately, she felt, in order to discountenance her, and so she threw back her head defiantly and greeted him coolly.

'Good morning, Mr. Devlin. You're better, I trust?'

He gave her a dry smile to acknowledge that her attitude had been noted and the message it conveyed understood. His answer, smoothly spoken, was a brief affirmative, and he set the direction their relationship was to take in stark relief when he continued with an abrupt:

'Right then, Miss Brent! Now that the formalities are over shall we begin?'

Mrs. Cherry, who had been fussing with the curtains while they fenced with each other, smiled upon them both with benign satisfaction and made to leave the room. She cautioned him with an admonitory finger before she left them together.

'Now remember what we agreed, Master Matthew. Two hours, and not a minute longer!'

He gave her a surprisingly boyish grin and shooed her out of the door. His smile, when he turned towards Nicola, had completely disappeared. He gave her a cursory glance as he headed for his desk and then began two hours of hectic activity.

Nicola revelled in it. At least when she was working at full speed she was spared the necessity of making conversation and no embarrassing silences were able to creep in to upset her new-found equilibrium.

In what seemed no time at all, Mrs. Cherry was back carrying a tray with coffee and biscuits. Matt Devlin lifted an impatient head from his desk when she interrupted them and scowled blackly at her when she planted herself firmly in front of him and ordered him to stop work immediately.

'Cherry, you're nothing but a confounded nuisance. You know I don't like to be fussed over when I'm working!'

'That may well be, Master Matthew, but Miss Brent here is entitled to a break if you aren't. So let's have no more scowls, if you don't mind. You'll have to give her a break or she'll collapse with fatigue!'

Nicola's hasty disclaimer was ignored by both of them. Mrs. Cherry's face relaxed into a grim smile when she saw that Matt Devlin was a little disconcerted to find the time had flown so quickly, wrapped up as he had been in his work, and she nodded with satisfaction when he apologized to Nicola for working her so hard.

'I'm terribly sorry, Miss Brent. I didn't realize how much work we'd got through. Of course you must have your coffee break. Bring the tray over here, Cherry, beside the window. I'll have mine here at my desk while I'm looking through these papers and perhaps you'll join Miss Brent while she has hers, to keep her company?'

Nicola, too, pressed her to stay, so she could hardly refuse. She poured out three cups and, when she had taken his over to his desk, sat down comfortably beside Nicola and helped herself liberally to sugar.

Nicola's relief at not having to share her coffee break with only Matt Devlin's disturbing presence was short-lived, for Mrs. Cherry's opening gambit made her stiffen with alarm, causing her to spill her coffee into her saucer. She tried to think up an answer that would mislead without her actually having to lie as she transferred her cup to a clean saucer. Frantically, her mind offered and rejected several possible answers in the space of a few seconds, but she could answer no less than the truth when Mrs. Cherry repeated her question.

'Where in Carswell are you living, Miss Brent?'

'Oh . . . er . . . I'm at Scaur Bank House with Mrs. Dawson, at present. But,' inspiration presented itself, 'I'm hoping to change, in a while, to a flat of my own.'

The subterfuge was well done. Mrs. Cherry, as she was intended to, took it to mean that she was lodging with Agnes Dawson as a temporary measure. She was not sure, however, how to take Mrs. Cherry's next remark.

'Hm . . . Agnes Dawson? Well, I'm sure you'll be glad to see the back of her! I didn't know she let off rooms, though. It's a bit of a comedown for my lady . . . !'

Nicola was spared the need of a reply when Matt
Devlin broke in with an observation of his own.

'Now, Cherry, that's enough gossip! I'm sure Miss
Brent isn't the least interested in your opinion of Mrs.
Dawson!'

Mrs. Cherry bridled. 'Gossip, Master Matthew?
Me, gossip?'

'Yes, Cherry. You do, you know. It's one of your
vices, but as you have so many virtues to outbalance it
we generally just ignore it . . . !'

Nicola chanced a look in his direction and was in time
to see his eyes dancing with mischief as he teased the old
lady; eyes that were quickly masked as he intercepted her
look.

Mrs. Cherry was outraged, but resignedly so, obviously
used to such remarks and able to take them with
equanimity. She must have felt, however, that some
umbrage was called for, for she turned her shoulder
away from him after casting him a withering look.

'Take no notice of him, Miss Brent. He just loves to
make me mad, but this time I refuse to be aggravated
into an argument. I always get the worst of it, anyway!'

Nicola could not help but recognize the deep bond of
affection that lay between the two, almost like that of
mother and son. She knew his remarks were made without fear of resentment or rancour on Mrs. Cherry's behalf
and she, in return, could answer him with the licence of
an old and devoted friend. How lovely, she thought, to
have a motherly person like Mrs. Cherry to take your
troubles to, and sighed a little at the thought of the scant
response she would receive from her Aunt Sarah in
similar circumstances.

Her troubles were not yet over, however, for when the
question of lunch was brought up she was once more on
the knife-edge of dilemma. Matt Devlin broached the
subject.

'Well, Cherry, if you've finished your chat perhaps we can get on with some more work before lunch?'

But Mrs. Cherry was firm. 'Indeed you can't, Master Matthew! You promised me you would stop after two hours, so your time is up! You can make your way back to your bed.'

Matt Devlin flushed a little with embarrassment at being chastised like a child, and before Nicola's amused gaze.

'Don't be ridiculous, Cherry,' he snapped irritably. 'I feel like working for another hour. At least until lunch-time.'

'You *promised*, Master Matthew . . . !'

Under Mrs. Cherry's adamant scrutiny he had to back down. Nicola had an inkling he was not as sorry as he proclaimed himself to be at having his work interrupted, for his pallor was even more pronounced than it had been earlier and he sank back in his chair and lit a cigarette with a gesture that indicated he had no more strength to argue.

'All right, Cherry, you win! I'll go quietly, but only on condition that Miss Brent stays for lunch and is here to start work again when I've had an hour's rest. Those are my conditions, and I'm sticking to them!'

She had to give in with a good grace. Turning to Nicola, she asked :

'Is that all right with you, Miss Brent? Or are you expected back for lunch?'

Nicola dearly wished she could have answered yes to that question, since she had no wish to lunch with the occupants of Blaise House, especially the son, but she had no option but to agree to stay, with Matt Devlin's slightly pleading look throwing her into confusion and Mrs. Cherry's conviction that his wish would be granted, plainly outlined on her cheery face.

'No, I'm not expected back,' she answered a trifle shortly. 'I can stay if you want me.'

'Good, then that's settled. I'll be ready to begin about three o'clock, Miss Brent. But anyway, I'll be downstairs for lunch today, so I'll let you know then what I want you to do this afternoon.'

Surely, Nicola thought frantically, there won't be just the two of us for lunch. I wonder if Mrs. Cherry eats with the family? Or if Charles Devlin is lunching at home? I don't think I could stand a *tête-à-tête* lunch. It would be just *too* much!

CHAPTER IX

LUNCH wasn't quite the ordeal she had expected it to be. When they had finished their coffee and Matt Devlin had retired to his room, Mrs. Cherry invited Nicola to look around the house and gardens for a while until she supervised the lunch. She was glad to accept, for she itched to examine the treasures she had glimpsed on her way upstairs earlier. She assured Mrs. Cherry that she would be able to amuse herself until the meal was ready and listened carefully to the housekeeper's instructions on how to find her way to the room where Mr. Charles's finest pieces were to be seen.

She was halted, however, before descending the fine old staircase, by the discovery of a small flight of stairs that led upwards to a gallery lined with portraits that she could only take to be of the Devlin ancestors.

She stepped hesitantly towards the first painting and gazed into eyes, masterfully executed on to canvas to give an uncannily mortal effect, that could only belong to someone akin to Matt Devlin. They had the same deep black depth, the fringe of eyelashes seeming almost thick enough to tangle, and set in a face moulded as his was around fine high cheekbones, and a strong, determined chin.

She lowered her eyes to the small bronze plaque at the foot of the portrait and stiffened instinctively as she read the name on it. Charles Devlin! With a sort of horrific, hypnotic power the portrait held her gaze. This, then, was the likeness of the man who was responsible for the tragedy that had disrupted her life! The man whose petty spite and jealousy had robbed her of her parents.

She was fired anew with the spirit of revenge that had first instigated her return to Carswell, to seek out, to unmask, and then finally to declare to the whole world the treachery of the Devlins of Scaur Bank Mills. She looked long and hard into the painted eyes, so like and yet so unlike Matt Devlin's, for there was none of Matt's vitality or even arrogance to be seen there, just a hint of sadness—or could it be remorse? Nicola asked herself bitterly. She contemplated the portrait and vowed to herself that justice would be done and his black deeds brought into the open so that everyone would know his true nature!

So absorbed was she that when a voice cut through her thoughts and spoke directly behind her she almost jumped from her skin.

'You must be Miss Brent . . .?'

She swung round to face the man who had spoken and reacted with an immediate shrinking away from the hand outstretched in greeting. It was Charles Devlin in the flesh! No mistaking his likeness to the portrait, even though he was now very much older. His hair, still thick and well-groomed, was amply sprinkled with grey, and fine lines crinkled the corners of his eyes as he smiled. The hint of melancholy she had noticed in the portrait was even more pronounced, although he was smiling at her with evident friendliness.

She took a hasty step backwards, leaving his extended hand in mid-air without acknowledging his greeting; her eyes enormous with the depth of feeling that swept her at the sight of him and of the memories he had resurrected. She saw bewilderment chase over his features at her reaction. The sheer horror stamped upon her face and her shrinking from physical contact, even to the extent of refusing to shake his hand, disturbed him greatly, but seconds later the bewilderment was chased from his face to be replaced by relief as he seemed to find an answer to her strange behaviour.

'My dear child, did I startle you? Fool that I am! I ought to have given more warning of my presence before confronting you like this. Please accept my apologies, my dear. I'm more sorry than I can say.'

Nicola pulled herself together. Her repugnance had to be overcome, or seemed to be overcome, if she were to get anywhere. There was no sense in antagonizing him. No. At this stage she needed to get his confidence, and her action of a few minutes ago was not the right way to go about it. So she managed to overcome her revulsion enough to take the hand still extended towards her with a show of amity that must have deceived him, for the worried look was replaced by one of pleasure and he moved forward a little so that her face, which was in the shadow, was more clearly revealed to him.

She heard his sharp breath of surprise and her eyebrows arched questioningly. He continued to stare, without speaking, until she began to feel uncomfortable. He still held her hand, so she gently disengaged her fingers from his clasp and searched desperately for words to break the silence between them.

Charles Devlin shook himself free of the spell that held him and ran his hand through his hair with a motion of perplexity. His voice when he spoke was husky and, it seemed to her, a little shocked.

'I'm sorry, my dear . . . for staring, I mean. It's just that, for a moment, you reminded me of someone I used to know . . . to love. It was your expression, I think . . . Or perhaps the shape of your mouth,' he shrugged his shoulders with a gesture of hopelessness and bent to peer more closely at her.

Nicola could not help but know that he was referring to her mother, for, whatever other faults he might have, it had been universally stated that he had never loved any other woman before or since. But this could not compensate for his black deeds, even if they had been motivated by love, and the throb of sympathy that had momentarily stirred her fled before the cold bare facts of his premeditated wickedness. She tried hard to repress a shiver, but he was quick to notice it. He exclaimed with alarm and self-condemnation :

'My dear, I really did give you a fright. You're as white as a sheet! Come, you're going downstairs with me to have a spot of brandy to take the chill from your bones. Matt will flay me alive if he finds out about my stupid behaviour, for he's been singing your praises for days now. He says you're the best secretary he's ever had, so he won't thank me for frightening the life out of you!'

Sheer surprise kept Nicola silent. Unprotestingly, she followed him to a small sitting-room on the ground floor where a large fire was burning in the open fireplace. Gently, he guided her to a comfortable armchair, then walked over towards a sideboard where there was an assortment of bottles and glasses. She leaned back against a cushion and let the warmth of the fire thaw the numbness from her limbs, numbness brought on, not as he had thought, by fright or cold, but by sheer strength of feeling against the man who, at that very moment, was leaning across with a smile of satisfaction to hand her a glass containing mellow amber liquid. She took it with a shaking hand and managed to return his smile. He sat back in the opposite chair and watched her as she sipped her drink, smiling a little at her shudder of distaste as the savage bite of the fiery liquid burned her tongue. She gasped and put down her glass, most of the contents still untouched.

'I see you don't appreciate my fine old Napoleon brandy,' he stated whimsically, raising his eyebrows in a way painfully reminiscent of his son Matthew.

Nicola found her voice at last. 'Oh, I do, Mr. Charles, but I must admit it's a little wasted on me as I'm not a sufficiently good judge. But I'm beautifully warm now.'

She stretched out her hands towards the glowing fire as she spoke and hoped its heat would account for the blush that was staining her cheeks. She was feeling unaccountably shy of the man who was regarding her with such approving kindliness and wished he would not look at her with such benevolence. Nicola found it hard to hate. She had tried to hate his son, only to find it an impossible task, but she had no wish to soften towards Charles Devlin, indeed she *mustn't* soften towards him, or she would be betraying her family as well as her own feelings.

Consequently, when he had assured himself that she had quite recovered from her fright and offered to show her his treasures, her voice showed none of the eager anticipation she felt at his invitation. He led the way to another room on the same floor and opened the door with a flourish. She saw, when she entered, that his pride was justified, because the room was a veritable storeroom of antiques, some rare, some beautiful, and all of them costly, as even her untrained eyes recognized. He led her first to a cabinet full of Chelsea pottery, then to one containing delicate Sèvres porcelain. On one wall was hung a Canaletto landscape, and on another a beautiful tapestry of great age; the colours muted and the design intricately lovely. She recognized a Van Dyck, and was inordinately pleased when Charles confirmed her estimate that a superb jewel cabinet standing in a corner beside the window was Buhl as being correct.

She was no expert, but she had an ingrained love of things old and lovely. In their quests around the antique shops, Liz and she had admired similar pieces to the ones in Charles Devlin's collection and had often sighed wistfully and enviously over them. The room was a treasure store; evidently the gathering of these pieces together had taken him most of his life and, judging by the light of pride in his eyes, had filled a want in him that badly needed to be assuaged.

He took her arm and gently guided her across to the window. A small table was set into the aperture. With the look of a conspiratorial child, he bent to take a drawer from the jewel cabinet and carried it over to the table. She watched him lay a piece of black velvet on the table, then, one by one, he produced for her inspection and admiration a series of rings, brooches, and other jewelled trinkets of breathtaking brilliance. She was dumb before such magnificence. Her expression spoke volumes, however, and Charles Devlin was in no doubt as to her appreciation. He picked out one particular piece and held it against her cheek. It was a superb emerald ring. A weak ray of winter sunshine filtered through the window and caught every facet of the stone as he stood back a little and turned it slightly, revelling in the glory of its animated beauty as it glittered a living green.

'I knew it!' he said in triumph. 'The very colour of your eyes, Miss Brent, and—dare an old man say it without offence—similar in nature?'

'In nature, Mr. Charles . . .?'

'Yes, my dear. Cool and distant until touched with the flame of love. See how this emerald springs to life under the sun's kiss, my dear. I've no doubt that when the right man comes along to awaken you from your spell you'll glow with a fire that will put this emerald to shame. I only wish,' he sighed deeply and heavily, 'that the person I bought this ring for could have lived to wear it for me . . . but it was not to be.'

She would have been less than human if she had not experienced a pang of pity as he stood gazing down at the ring, lost in what were obviously unhappy memories of the woman he had loved so very much. His shoulders drooped as she watched and as his head bent over the drawer to replace the jewel she saw a suspicious brightness reflected in his eyes. She looked away quickly, hating to intrude on his grief, and swallowed to try to disperse the ache in her throat.

Mrs. Cherry's hearty voice broke in on the poignant moment. Nicola turned to her with relief as she entered the room and smiled brightly to disguise the wistful droop of her mouth.

'There now! I thought I'd find you in here. Dinner's ready, Mr. Charles. I'll just bang the gong to let Master Matthew know, and if you'll go into the dining-room I'll tell Doris to begin serving.'

'Thank you, Cherry,' Charles Devlin now had complete control of his emotions, 'we'll do just that.'

He turned to Nicola with a smile and held out his arm to lead her to the dining-room. She took it diffidently; her pulses had leapt at the mention of Matt Devlin's name, and she had to struggle to compose her expression to one of calmness. Charles Devlin placed her to the left of him at the table and when Matt entered the room, seconds later, he took the seat directly opposite.

He was fully dressed and looked more like the man she was accustomed to seeing around the office. His father glanced rather worriedly at his still-pale face, but evidently decided against mentioning the fact that he looked far from well. When the soup had been served, he broke the silence that had descended upon them at Matt's entrance by telling him how Nicola and he had spent the last hour.

'I've been showing Miss Brent my collection, Matt. I think she's enjoyed seeing it.' He raised an inquiring eyebrow in her direction.

'I most certainly have, Mr. Charles,' she avoided looking in Matt's direction. 'I think it's fabulous! It must be very valuable.'

'Hm . . . yes. But that is rather a sore subject between Matt and me at present, my dear. I'm afraid he thinks I'm rather extravagant. Not that I don't see your point, Matt,' he hurried on before his son could interrupt, 'but I must admit that having spent my life building up my collection I'll find it rather hard to stop myself from buying other pieces when the opportunity arises and I see something that takes my fancy.'

Matt broke in before his father could say any more. With a hard look in his direction he reproved him :

'I hardly think this is a proper time to discuss it, Father. I'm sure Miss Brent isn't interested in our personal affairs.'

'Nonsense, my boy! You said yourself she's a good secretary, and a good secretary never repeats anything she hears about her employer's affairs. Besides, I'm sure Miss Brent would be able to put forward some ideas of her own for dealing with our problem, if you give her the opportunity. There's nothing to beat women's intuition, and sometimes, if we're too near to a problem, we find it hard to see a solution that might be under our noses.'

Matt pushed away his plate with an impatient hand. He was annoyed, Nicola could tell, for when he raised her bewildered eyes to his they were bright with irritation, and she looked down at her hands rather than see the anger which she felt was directed at her as well as his father.

'I'm quite sure Miss Brent has affairs of her own to keep her occupied without burdening her with ours. As for intuition . . .' his tone was enigmatical, 'I must confess that I haven't found intuition to be her strong point, up to now !'

Nicola framed an indignant reply. She felt sure he was making an oblique reference to their last meeting in his office and her attitude to his advances, but she could not defend herself against such an intangible charge. How, she wondered, had she lacked intuition at that encounter? It had so clearly been a spark of opportunism on his part to take advantage, as he had, of her momentary weakness in the face of what had been an interlude of emotional strife. So she had to content herself with a glare of indignation that caused him to do no more than raise his eyebrows in the hatefully derogatory way she had come to associate with him.

Charles, quite oblivious to the undercurrents between them, carried on with his theme. He turned to Nicola, ignoring Matt's frown, and asked her :

'How much do you know about the trouble we have been having lately, Miss Brent?'

Nicola hesitated. She knew he was referring to the enormous amount of sub-standard material that was being rejected daily by the examiners in the factory. Some days before Matt's illness he had called a meeting of the heads of the departments to try to sort out the reason for the apparent lack of interest in their work that the younger element amongst the staff had been showing to a marked degree for some months past. Yards and yards of printed material had been thrown to one side as waste because of some slight faults that were evidently caused through carelessness or sheer indifference on the part of the young workers, who, when reprimanded by their foremen, either shrugged their shoulders with a couldn't-care-less attitude or tried to put the blame on their machines or any other element that might have a bearing on the damage.

She had listened as Matt had stressed the urgency of cutting out the needless waste of time and material to the men in charge and could not help but sympathize with them when they had trooped out of the office with long faces, after reiterating that they would try again to get through to their workers, but knowing full well that their pleas would fall on deaf ears. Matt had not been satisfied to leave all the spadework to these men, however, and had himself gone down to the weaving sheds to talk to the youngsters in person to try to get them interested in the job they were doing. He hadn't talked down to them, but had spoken to them as equals explaining in detail the cut-throat competition their firm was up against and the vital need to cut their margin of profit in order to compete with larger combines. But all the response he had had was sullen silence from the young lads and giggling from the girls.

One of the work's foremen, Garry Hately, a forceful, no-nonsense type of the old school, had advocated sacking half a dozen or more of the worst offenders as an example to the others to pull their socks up, but Matt would have none of it. The youngsters, he had insisted, were needed in order to fulfil their orders. They had had full and expensive training and he looked to them to carry on working for the firm for many years to come. To Hately's comment that they were more bother than they were worth he had defended the youngsters by saying that they were going through a stage of teenage malaise that was affecting all of their generation and that they would grow out of it, given time, and turn out to be as good or even better workers than their fathers and mothers before them. Hately's reply to that had been a hoot of derisive laughter that had annoyed Matt intensely, and he had silenced the man by stating his admiration of a generation who refused to be browbeaten and who reacted far more quickly to reason than to intimidation.

'The days of serfdom have gone for ever, Hately,' he had witheringly decreed, 'and I, for one, am not sorry!' Hately had left the room in a huff, then, but as he went he was heard to mutter, 'And only time will tell which of us is right, Mr. Almighty Devlin!'

An idea had sprung into Nicola's mind the following day. She had chewed it over, trying to decide whether to offer it as a solution to the problem, but had decided against it, more on the grounds of being a traitor to her own cause than the fact that he might reject her idea with one of his amused grins.

She realized, with a jolt, that they were both waiting for an answer to the question she had been asked, Charles with an indulgent smile and Matt with a look of bored indifference. She gritted her teeth with annoyance at his obvious doubts regarding her ability to help and directed her answer to Charles.

'I know quite a bit about the difficulties in the works, Mr. Charles. I didn't realize, of course, the full extent of the damage being done until I heard your remarks about cutting down on your hobby and I hope it won't be necessary for you to deny yourself the pleasure of carrying on with it. If things *are* as serious as you imply,' she looked at Matt then with a definite challenge, 'then perhaps you might be interested in a scheme I've thought up.'

Charles leaned forward eagerly, encouraging her to continue. She waited for some response from Matt, but was disappointed; he merely tipped back his chair and sat balancing on it with an air of patient resignation as if he could not wait for her to get it over. With heightened colour, she addressed her remarks to Charles.

'The way I see it is this. You've tried to get the young girls and boys interested in a job that is both repetitious and boring, and failed. You know yourself that today's children need more incentive to work than their parents did. It's not enough to tell them to do a job, you must make them *want* to do it.' She received a nod of agreement from Charles and was encouraged to go on. 'Well, why not make the job a bit more glamorous? Encourage them to see it as a job they can boast to their friends about! How many of them, for instance, know that the material they spend hours over each day ends up as a finished product being worn at, say, a film première, for example? How many of them know that they make material for the great fashion houses that are household names, such as Balenciaga, Balmain, Dior, Cardin, Chanel, Castillo, Givenchy, Lanvin, Ricci, St. Laurent . . .?' She paused through sheer lack of breath and saw she had them both interested. Charles was openly agog, and Matt slowly let his chair down to rest on its four legs, his eyes never leaving her face, and breathed softly, 'Go on . . .'

Feeling terribly self-conscious with his gaze firmly riveted on her face, she continued: 'Well, there isn't much more to it, really. As I see it, all you have to do is find a way to bring these facts to the notice of the young-sters and matters will resolve themselves. After all, what girl could resist making sure that the material she is working on is no less than perfect if she thinks it might end up as a dress for her favourite actress, or even one of the Royal Family?'

Charles smacked the palms of his hands together jubilantly and cried out, 'She's got it! I do believe she's come up with the answer!'

Matt waved him to silence, his glance not wavering from her face, and asked her cautiously:

'And how do you propose we get these facts over with as much glamour as you suggest, Miss Brent? Have booklets printed . . .? I doubt if they would even bother to read them. Have a film show, perhaps . . .? Again, they wouldn't bother to come. So how . . .?'

'Get real, live models, wearing creations made from your own materials, and put on a show in the works' canteen during the lunch hour when they'll all be there! Give it the whole works—a commentator, painted back-

cloths, a portable organ for background music, the lot!
I'm sure it'll work!'

Matt expelled a slow breath and sat back slowly. She
waited for him to tear her idea to pieces with his sarcastic
wit and found herself twisting her fingers together under
the table as she anticipated his ridicule. His reply was
typical, and more or less what she had expected. Silently,
she prayed for control as his mocking words dropped into
the silence that had fallen. Turning slightly, as if to
address his father, but keeping his eyes upon Nicola's
tense face, he accepted her idea as sound but at the same
time infuriated her by his bland innuendo.

'It seems as if Miss Brent has indeed hit upon a solution to our difficulties, and I congratulate her. We must
also thank her for her consideration, for she seems to
have our interests at heart to a far greater degree than
any other of our employees. I think,' he threw a quick
grin in his father's direction, 'you must have charmed
her, for I'm under no illusion as to her opinion of me,
but then,' his sharp glance bored into Nicola, 'I haven't
yet had the opportunity of gathering together a valuable
collection of trinkets, and it *has* been said that "silent
jewels do more than quick words to move a woman's
mind." '

CHAPTER X

CHARLES, taking Matt's remark as being meant lightly, laughed delightedly, and Nicola, though fuming, thought it politic to ignore it rather than be made to look foolish by objecting to what she knew Matt would claim was intended as a joke. So, after throwing him a look of mute fury, she pointedly ignored him for the rest of the meal. She ploughed through peach-baked gammon, followed by a luxurious-looking sweet Mrs. Cherry called Raspberry Alaska, and tasted none of it. She grimly resisted entering into the discussion going on between Matt and his father as to how and when the idea could be put into practice and had to force herself to answer when Matt, a bland, unrepentant Matt, asked her point-blank if she could offer any suggestions as to where they could apply for the required models. She grudgingly told him that she could arrange for some of her friends from London to carry out the job, knowing that they would be delighted to take part if only to come to Carswell with all expenses paid to see her for a few hours. He told her to go ahead and make all the arrangements necessary, so she made a mental reservation to phone Liz that evening to find out who she could book, and when, and gave him a cool nod to acknowledge his request.

Charles, seemingly oblivious to the tension between them, insisted on sending for a bottle of champagne to launch the forthcoming event, as he termed it, and as they stood with glasses raised for the toast, he turned to Nicola and said simply, 'To Nicola.'

Her eyes dared Matt to second it and she could have stamped her foot with temper when he raised his glass to her with ironic solemnity and repeated, 'To Nicola,' before throwing back his head and swallowing the contents in one gulp. She turned to Charles and protested:

'But aren't you being rather premature? Surely we should wait to find out whether the idea is a success before letting our enthusiasm run away with us?'

Charles pooh-poohed the idea. 'Of course it will be a success! It's such a marvellous scheme it can't fail, don't you agree, Matt?'

Before he could answer, Nicola said coldly: 'I'm sure Mr. Devlin would have come up with an equally good idea, given ti...'

Without allowing her to finish, Charles broke in.

'Oh, I say, Nicola, we can't have you calling us Mr., now. We wouldn't dream of addressing you as Miss Brent, you are Nicola to us, and we would deem it an honour if you would call us by name,' he turned to his son for confirmation, 'wouldn't we, Matt?'

'But of course,' Matt answered smoothly, meeting the challenge in her eyes with amusement. 'After all, we are friends, aren't we?'

Although she knew only too well that he was being sarcastic, her blood ran cold as she realized just how far her enthusiasm had led her. Friends! How could she call either of them friend, least of all *Charles* Devlin? In the excitement of the past few minutes her role of avenger had been swallowed up in the furore her rash suggestions had heralded. Charles was beaming at her, confident that she had their best interests at heart, and eager to welcome her into their circle, and now she could think of no way back to the aloof reserve she had practised in their company. She turned away on the pretence of putting down her glass in order to avoid answering, but Matt followed her to the window where she stood gazing with blank eyes at the sweep of lawn outside and startled her by whispering in her ear:

'Couldn't you play up, if only to please my father? I promise you,' the mocking note was again evident in his voice, 'that I won't take it as a gesture of surrender if you'll force yourself to call me Matt, even though,' he hooked his finger under her chin and glinted at her, 'all the time you are play-acting I'll be wishing you were serious!'

She wanted to make some clever, dampening reply, but the old magic was working on her like a charm. The feelings she had kept damped down with rigid self-control were being forced to the surface once again by his fascinating charm. His *deliberate* charm, she told herself fiercely. Don't fool yourself that you're the only girl to be subjected to his magnetic appeal; he uses it to further his own ends, you silly idiot, don't let him see you're susceptible!

She managed a nonchalant shrug and the look she turned on him when she answered was cool in the extreme.

'I suppose that, working together as we do, it would be silly to keep up an atmosphere of strife, as, besides hindering our work, it's wearing on the nerves. Friendliness is the only answer in the circumstances, so let's say then that we're friends . . . Matt.'

He quirked a black eyebrow at her as she met his eyes and then gave a slight bow as if to concede her victory. Then he suddenly seemed to tire of the verbal thrust and parry, for he swung away from the window to put down his glass on the table. Her eyes flickered over his face and she felt a pang as she registered that it looked as pale and drawn as it had when she arrived that morning. He swiftly excused himself to his father and left the room without a backward glance. Her treacherous heart leapt with compassion and she had to hold herself firmly in check in order to resist the temptation to run after him, but the mad impulse passed and she sank down wearily on to a chair.

Charles, too, looked worried. He took a few steps towards the door as if to follow him, then changed his mind and looked inquiringly at Nicola. She stared back at him, wondering if the effect of her thumping heart and dry mouth showed in her face, but was reassured when Charles shook his head sadly and admitted :

'I did the wrong thing in allowing you to come here today, Nicola. I let Matt overrule me, against my better judgement. He's still shaky from that bout of 'flu and the work has been too much for him, I'm afraid.'

Nicola mumbled her agreement.

'However,' Charles decided firmly, 'he won't get his own way tomorrow ! No more work for that young man until the doctor says so !' She hoped the thankfulness she felt was not reflected in her face, for she was dreading the idea of returning the next day to face yet another battle of wills as seemed fated to happen each time they met. Gratefully, she heard Charles express the view that it would be wise if she were to call it a day and that he would ring for his chauffeur to take her home immediately.

The car was brought round to the front door and Charles helped her into it. He instructed the chauffeur to take her straight home and saw to it himself that the rug was wrapped carefully round her knees, even though the car heater worked perfectly and her journey was comparatively short. She wondered, in the back of her mind, why she didn't cringe from his touch—why, when he spoke to her so kindly, she responded instead of being repulsed. She felt confused and unhappy. She should hate them both, but instead, she felt a warming towards one and—though she had faced the fact squarely and thought she had come to terms with it the knowledge still frightened her—she loved the other !

As the car drew away she waved mechanically to Charles, then, as he disappeared from view, she sank back against the soft upholstery and closed her eyes to give herself up to blank misery.

Her aunt was home when the car stopped outside the house. She opened the front door for Nicola, her eyes popping with unashamed curiosity at the sight of the opulent car and uniformed chauffeur. When Nicola had satisfied her curiosity as to its owner and what she had been doing at Blaise House, she was amazed at the surge of partisanship she felt when Sarah began libelling the Devlins with vitriolic relish. She just couldn't stand to hear another thing about them and their doings, so she excused herself quickly and ran to the sanctuary of her room.

Later that evening, she made the promised phone call to Liz. When the preliminaries had been disposed of, she explained to her friend the reason for her unexpected call. Liz, as she had foreseen, was delighted.

'You mean you want me to bring some of the girls up there to put on a show for the *beast*?' she yelled down the phone with gleeful relish.

Nicola winced at her description of Matt, but could hardly censure her; she had been the one, after all, who had given him that title so it behove her to eradicate the impression from her friend's mind.

'Oh, Liz, don't call him that! He *is* my employer, and it might slip out when you meet him. Besides . . .' her voice trailed away reluctantly.

'Besides what?' Liz prompted.

'Well . . . he is beastly, but I don't think he could be described *as* a beast, if you know what I mean?'

'Yes, I think so,' Liz replied thoughtfully.

Nicola was sure she didn't, but she decided not to pursue the matter, Liz being a genius for prying things out of her that she didn't want her to know. She carried on firmly before Liz could ask any more pertinent questions.

'About this show. Can you scout around and find out which of the girls will be free at the same time as yourself and let me know as soon as possible?'

Liz assured her she would do everything she could to help and promised to phone her back immediately she had a definite date fixed with the girls they had in mind. Before ringing off, Nicola asked her anxiously :

'Is there any improvement in the state of affairs between yourself and Dulcie? I wrote her a really stinging letter threatening her with all kinds of reprisals if she didn't start to pull her weight in the flat and keep decent hours. Has it had any effect?'

Liz wasn't making the same mistake as last time. She gave a happy-sounding laugh that was culled up solely to reassure Nicola—which it did. Not for the world would she inform her of the pitched battles that raged practically every evening in the flat. Dulcie was idle and impudent and Liz was containing herself with as much patience as she could muster until the day she could welcome Nicola back to the flat and send Dulcie on her way without a shred of regret.

'Nicola love, don't you worry about Dulcie, she's having a whale of a time here in London and things are much better since you told her off, honestly.'

Nicola put the phone down, reassured. She would write to Dulcie that same night, she told herself, and tell her to keep up the good work.

After that, the project simply snowballed. It was very soon evident to everyone concerned that the canteen was not going to be big enough to hold everyone who wanted tickets for the show. Once it had got around that there were to be real, live models from London wearing dresses made of *their* material, the youngsters scrambled for tickets for themselves and their mothers, sisters, and aunties. Everybody, it seemed, was determined to be there. Matt had returned to work, but the office routine was upset by all the arrangements that had to be made for the gala evening. They were back to the stage of chilly politeness; a little advanced, perhaps, in that he now called her Nicola instead of Miss Brent and she returned the compliment by addressing him by his first name when they were alone, as he had instigated the day she was at Blaise House. Though she would dearly have loved to ignore the promise she had made, she hadn't the nerve to go back to calling him Mr. Matt, except in front of Jessica or any other of the staff.

She was sitting frowning over a list of couturiers who might be persuaded to let them have some of their dresses on loan for that one evening, when her buzzer went, indicating she was wanted in the inner office. When she went in Matt was pacing the floor. He looked up eagerly as she opened the door.

'Oh, there you are, Nicola.'

She wondered at the pleased smile on his face, and was as excited as he when he explained :

'We can forget our worries about the canteen not being big enough. I've managed to persuade the manager of the Galaxy to let us have his place for the night. It should be spacious enough, don't you think? And as there's a stage there, we won't have to worry about erecting a platform and such-like as we were intending to do in the canteen.' She clasped her hands together with happy relief at the news, her eyes shining with enthusiasm.

'Oh, that's wonderful! The Galaxy? Isn't that the grand new dance hall that's been built in town? The one the girls in the factory flock to on a Saturday night?'

He smiled with satisfaction at her reaction. 'Yes, and do you want to know something else?'

'Oh, what?' She took hold of his sleeve in her eagerness.

'It has a bar! Two bars, in fact. So our worries are resolved in respect of what refreshments to provide. Jock Blain, the manager, has offered to provide staff to run the bars, one for soft drinks and the other for cocktails—*and*,' he had kept his best bit of news till the last, 'the local television studios are interested! They want to run a programme on the show and say they'll provide all the lighting and sets, so we're all ready to go. This idea of yours seems to be a sure-fire winner, I must admit!'

Her hand, which had quite involuntarily clutched at his sleeve while he was talking, was suddenly still as he laughed down at her glowing face. He tensed, their eyes clung and her laughter faded to a softly-drawn breath as his arm under her fingers went rigid. She sensed, too late, in the leashed strength of him a primitive emotion and was caught up in the reckless tide that swept him. Seconds later, she felt his lips on hers, savagely demanding her surrender. She held on desperately to her swimming senses and managed to strain her lithe body a fraction away from his. His lips still clung to hers as if he could not taste enough of their sweetness, willing her to respond, and almost succeeding. For a long wavering moment the kiss lasted, and when he lifted his head to glitter down at her she slumped against him, spent with feeling.

His voice was a cool contrast to the fervour that flickered in his eyes as he whispered close to her ear:

'Why do you fight me? Relax. I won't bite you, Coppernob.'

This last teasing endearment pierced the cocoon of bemused rapture that had her in its grip. From afar she heard that whispered, 'Coppernob'. It seemed to her tortured conscience like a voice from the dead, her mother's voice, calling her by the pet name she had used to her as a child. She stiffened within the circle of his arms and, her voice choked with tears, she managed to utter:

'Leave me alone! Don't touch me! I hate you, Matt Devlin!'

He took a step away from her, letting his arms slide from her waist, and protested with a slight smile which, nevertheless, did not quite reach his eyes.

'Oh, come now, Nicola. You *hate* me . . .?' He gave her trembling mouth a tender flick at the corner with the tip of his finger and let his eyes linger where his lips had kissed so passionately a few seconds before. She knew he was unconvinced. Girls fell so easily into his trap he could perhaps be forgiven for thinking she was putting on an act so as to whet his appetite, but this time he would have to be convinced, because she knew she could not withstand him if he had to really put his mind to storming the pitifully frail barriers she tried to hide behind.

She whipped up her anger and forced herself to remember all the things she had to hold against him. Dulcie's dismissal, the fact that he was Charles Devlin's son, his despicable treatment of her that first day in the hut—she marshalled them all to her defence to give authenticity to her words. In a ringing voice, full of contempt, she shot at him:

'What makes you think I could ever find you attractive, Matt Devlin? An arrogant, conceited brute who thinks nothing of molesting a defenceless girl on a solitary walk! A . . .'

Before she could get in another word, he protested:

'I explained about that . . .!'

Swiftly, before he could argue, her words tumbled out:

'. . . A man who gives his word easily and then breaks it easier still. "Please stay on, Miss Brent, and I promise that if you remain in my employment you'll have no complaint about my future conduct," ' she mimicked. From the start he gave she realized that shot had gone home and she hurried on before her courage failed her.

'And then on another occasion you stated convincingly that anything between us would be strictly business. And now this . . .! You seem to spend most of your time forcing your unwelcome attentions upon your female employees. You're no gentleman! You're not even a man of your word! No, Mr. Devlin, when I want someone to make love to me I'll choose a man I can respect and trust, not an arrogant bully!'

She finished on a high quavering note that sounded to her own ears like the beginning of a hysterical scream. Appalled, she waited for his wrath to fall on her head, but his calm, controlled tone, with its undercurrent of ice, was a complete anti-climax. As she heard his words she could have congratulated herself on having made her goal, for his distaste was underlined by each stinging sentence.

'That's enough, Miss Brent! You've made your point! I have quite a clear picture of myself, as seen through your eyes, and if that's the way you see me then I have every sympathy with your point of view. But, at the risk of being accused once more of being less than a gentleman, may I remind you that on the last occasion when I *forced* my attentions upon you you seemed, at first, a very willing victim.'

She flushed angrily and tried to interrupt, but he waved her to silence.

'It's all right, I've no intention of holding an inquest, but just remember this. If you don't want to be noticed, you would be wise to get rid of the provocative outfits you prance about the office in, stop looking at every man in your vicinity with the expression of a sexy cherub, and climb behind some horn-rimmed spectacles and a pair of highly respectable thick, lisle stockings . . .!'

At her outraged gasp, he looked her up and down before dismissing her with a last laconic remark.

'As a secretary, Miss Brent, you fulfil all your promises, but as a woman . . .'

His casually shrugged shoulders were meant to convey that words failed him, but Nicola, incited by his derogatory reference to her femininity, was not to be put off. Through clenched teeth, she demanded that he finish his sentence.

'Yes, as a woman . . .?'

He met her brilliantly angry eyes with derision in his own and finished his remark with cool cheek.

'. . . You're a cheat!'

Her ears caught a trace of amusement in his voice and she looked at him aghast. He returned her look with a devilish glint that told her that she was right, he *was* laughing at her. It was an unkind, mocking laughter that seared her sensitive feelings and made her wonder if she really had made a mistake in her judgement of him, or, if perhaps his heartlessness was a cloak to hide his chagrin. Suddenly it all seemed unbearable. She wanted to get away; she *had* to get away from his unnerving presence. Quick tears spurted to her eyes and she turned away hastily lest he should see them. She sped from him, through her own office and past a startled Jessica, to the door that led to the main exit. She ran towards her aunt's house and up the path to the front door. Tears blinded her as she fumbled with the catch and almost fell over a rapturous Rufus who had raced towards the front of the house as soon as he heard her at the door. She leaned against the wall and prepared to give herself up to the tears that were forcing their way between her downcast lashes. A slight sound from upstairs told her that her aunt was in the vicinity and she jerked away from the wall and opened the door to race down the path, an excited dog at her heels, before Sarah could detain her with her endless questions.

For once, she saw nothing of the beauty of the fells in the background or the ever-changing character of the river. She stumbled on for miles and finally threw herself down, exhausted, on a grassy bank to weep at last, in complete privacy. Through the agony of her heartbreak, she could hear her own voice saying to him, 'I hate you, Matt Devlin', and she wept anew for the torment of a heart that was crying out in angry dismay, *'I love you, Matt Devlin!'*

CHAPTER XI

LIZ swept on to the stage with exaggerated aplomb, and was greeted by tumultuous applause from the audience, mostly comprising young weavers and printers and their families, as they voiced their appreciation of her highly sophisticated image and of the exotic evening trouser suit in vivid pink, blue and purple nylon that she was displaying with such devastating effect.

The show was well and truly launched and, judging by the audience's reaction as each model appeared on the stage to delight them with a succession of stunning outfits, was an unqualified success. Nicola sat in the front row beside Charles Devlin. She was achingly conscious of the empty seat next to hers that had been reserved for Matt but which was, as yet, unoccupied. Aline Royston was sitting at the other side of the empty seat and was making no secret of the fact that she was annoyed at Matt's absence. Every now and then she would twist around to look towards the back of the large ballroom, now packed to capacity with rows of chairs to accommodate the audience, towards the door which Matt must enter by when he eventually arrived.

Nicola forced herself not to follow her example. Her pulses were hammering at the anticipation of their forthcoming meeting; the first since the day she had run out of his presence to find what comfort she could from tramping the countryside until she had been on the verge of collapse. Some merciful providence had decreed that Matt had to rush away that same afternoon on urgent business and she had reached the office the following morning to find Charles in charge. The relief had been almost overwhelming. Thankfully, she had thrown herself into the work of organizing the show, displaying an attention to detail that had amazed Charles, so much so that he had felt bound to protest.

'Nicola, my dear, you ought to slow down a little. I don't want you to run yourself into the ground as you are doing. Everything will get done, slowly but surely, and I most certainly don't want Matt blaming me for tiring you out. This business he's about will mean that a lot of work will fall on your shoulders when he returns, and if he comes back to find you exhausted he'll vent his ire on me, and *that* I have no wish to endure.'

He had smiled at her as he spoke, but she had known him to be genuinely concerned for her welfare, so had slackened her pace a little in order to ease his mind. She had had no idea, and had hesitated to ask Charles, when he would be returning, and it was not until the day of the show that Charles had sent her pulses leaping by saying :

'Matt is coming home tonight, Nicola, so we'll have to make sure to reserve him a seat beside us. He doesn't give the exact time of his arrival, but he assures me he'll be here before the finale.' Nicola muttered something about being pleased he wasn't going to miss it and Charles, too wrapped up in last-minute details to notice her lack of enthusiasm, heartily agreed.

They had been kept busy right up to the opening, and now that the event was upon them Nicola wanted to relax with justifiable pride in a job well done, but her nerves were stretched to breaking point as the moment of their meeting drew nearer.

Liz had brought six girls with her and they were all staying at Blaise House, at Charles's insistence. The greatest surprise of all, to Nicola, had been the appearance of Jimmy Sorenson, an old friend of hers who, in the past, had made it clear that he would have liked to be much more than a friend but had eventually come to realize, without actually giving up hope, that Nicola, although heartwhole, was never likely to regard him as anything but a very good pal. He had joined the party in the role of organizer and commentator, a job he was well qualified to do, but he, as well as the rest of the party, knew that his prime interest had been in meeting Nicola once again. Their first meeting, when Nicola had met them at the railway station, had made it obvious that Jimmy's hopes were still running high and the girls, in their open, teasing way, had ribbed her unmercifully about him. Nicola, well used to this kind of ribbing and knowing it to be good-natured and free from malice, had withstood it smilingly, and after extricating herself from his enthusiastic embrace she hadn't had the heart to chide him for acting in a manner that was as normal to him as eating and drinking.

As he was an unexpected guest and no provision had been made for him at Blaise House, she had persuaded her aunt to put him up. Sarah hadn't been keen, when first approached by Nicola, but when she had been assured that no extra work would be put on her shoulders and that Nicola herself intended to see to his meals and launder the sheets when he had gone, she capitulated. Her hypocritical manner when Jimmy had thanked her for allowing him to stay had angered Nicola, and she had bitten her lip as she heard Sarah say to Jimmy that of course she was glad to welcome one of her niece's oldest friends. Jimmy was naturally delighted to be so near to Nicola and she, lonely and glad of his uncomplicated friendship, was glad to have him with her.

A tremendous burst of applause brought Nicola to earth. As she focused her mind upon the stage she felt a thrill of pride at the pure professionalism displayed by her friends as they danced, pirouetted and floated across the stage in their colourful outfits. She heard Jimmy enthuse through the microphone.

'And this, ladies and gentlemen, is Rita, wearing a go-anywhere-at-any-time dress of creaseless Tricel jersey in bright orange, pink and yellow, manufactured, of course, by yourselves!'

A chorus of catcalls and whistles followed Rita's exit from the stage. Next came Doreen, in a dinner dress made of uncrushable Banlon jersey in an exotic deep pink, green, and blue print designed by Aline Royston, which brought a pleased smile to her face as Jimmy commented on the fact that the designer was sitting in the front row. Moira tripped on in a dress he described as a practised traveller—firm heavy cotton in deep red, splashed with vivid pink and orange, cut to an easy A-line, cool and sleeveless, and with tiny brass buttons. But the star of the show was, without any doubt, Mirabelle. Nicola had followed her career with interest, and was more than pleased to see that the young West Indian girl was firmly on the ladder of success. Her dark skin showed up to perfection the vivid colours that were so much in vogue with the younger set. She seemed almost to burst with vitality when she made her entrance—not walking or slinking, as the other girls did, but literally dancing on in time to the background music and communicating to the audience an immense enthusiasm for life and the job she was doing so well. They loved her, and their unstinting applause each time she appeared stimulated her efforts to a peak of perfection seldom seen even in the salons of the great fashion houses. When the curtain fell for the first half of the programme the applause was deafening, but exhilarating.

In the midst of the laughing, clapping throng Nicola missed the small commotion Matt made as he slipped into the seat beside her. Her first intimation that he was present was Aline Royston's pleased voice saying, 'Matt darling ...!'

Instinctively she tensed, then, without delay, turned in

her seat and began an animated conversation with Charles who was, as yet, unaware of his son's arrival. She was drawn into Charles's circle of friends who were assured that she was responsible for the whole idea, and suffered the embarrassment of being praised to the skies and of having to linger among her admirers rather than turn to confront the man whose magnetic presence was making itself felt even through the babbling of countless voices.

She heard Aline Royston's tinkling laughter ring out and relaxed a little, thinking his attention was completely occupied, then was nonplussed to feel his hand on her arm—she had no doubt it was his, for no one else had the power to send the blood singing in her ears at a touch—and his coolly formal voice saying:

'You've done a marvellous job, Miss Brent. It's a terrific success and we owe it all to your efforts.'

She turned her head to find him leaning close and their faces almost touched. He regarded her steadily, his lips unsmiling, and she was utterly confused, so much so that she found herself stuttering slightly as she thanked him. He seemed relieved to find she was prepared to behave as if everything was normal between them and his firm lips quirked a little in a wry smile before he turned his attention to an impatient Aline.

She must have been listening, for Nicola heard her ask Matt:

'Matt darling, how can you possibly know what the show is like, you've only just arrived?'

Nicola unashamedly eavesdropped as he answered:

'I've driven like fury to get here before the show finished. As it happened I arrived a few minutes after the opening, but I've been standing at the back so as not to disturb everyone by making for my seat in the middle of it.'

By this time Charles had noticed him and he, too, had

his quota of questions to be answered, so Aline had to take a back seat while Matt answered his father's queries. The interval gave her time to think. She had missed nothing of the momentary encounter between Nicola and Matt, and her intuition rang a warning bell as she pondered on the strain between them. Strain, she reasoned, meant that at some time or other there had been a clash of personalities, and she was alive to the danger of Matt seeing his secretary as a person and not simply an appendage to his office. To Aline's one-track mind the indication was obvious. Nicola was trying to inveigle her way into Matt's life. She drew in a sharp breath at the thought. Matt was *her* property! She had every intention of seeing to it that he proposed, sooner or later, and had been quite content to bide her time; confident that no one in her immediate vicinity offered any kind of competition. But now . . . !

The second half of the show was devoted to colour films of celebrities and stars of the theatre and cinema world at glittering functions, quite a few of whom were wearing dresses of materials easily recognizable by the excited youngsters who were avidly watching. During one part of the programme in which a member of the Royal Family was shown enjoying recreation, a voice pitched high with amazement was heard from the back of the hall to say:

'Hey, that dress that she's wearing is one of *my* jobs! You remember it, Linda, it's number AJC79!'

The rest of the audience roared with laughter at this little cameo, but it showed the members of the management and staff that the object of the show was being realized. The message was being received and understood.

When the curtain went down for the last time, and the girls had paraded before a storm of clapping and whistling workers, there was a mad scramble to the bars for refreshments. People formed into groups to discuss the evening's entertainment and Nicola was beseiged with congratulations. Charles, especially, was delighted, and made no secret of the fact that the show owed its success to Nicola's efforts and that it had been her idea, initially. She glowed with pleasure and found herself surrounded by a laughing, congratulatory crowd. Even Matt's eyes, as she looked towards him, were full of pleasure, and he gave her a 'thumbs up' sign over the heads of the people around her. The gesture was so spontaneous that when he reached her side shortly afterwards and professed himself well pleased with her efforts she felt a glow encompass her at the genuine warmth of his voice.

Aline Royston bit her lip with annoyance. She was unused to being pushed into the background and it was an experience she found extremely distasteful. She hooked her arm around Matt's in an intimate gesture and proclaimed loudly for the benefit of those close by:

'Matt darling, I think we've done our duty by the workers now, don't you? And you did promise to take me to the Huntsman, remember? I'd like to go now!'

Matt regarded her with unconcealed annoyance. Her flagrant bad manners had embarrassed everyone within earshot, but Aline didn't seem to care. She stood tapping her foot with evident boredom and waited for his answer.

Just then Liz, accompanied by Jimmy and the girls, came clattering down the steps from the stage dressed in their own clothes and in obviously high spirits. Liz hailed Nicola and she turned towards her voice to greet her, but before Liz reached her side Jimmy put on a spurt and ran to lift her from her feet to twirl her around the room with laughing exuberance, regardless of the number of eyes that watched them. Matt was watching, too. She sensed his narrow-eyed stare even before Jimmy ceased his foolery and deposited her back at his side. To cover up her loss of dignity, Nicola began introducing Jimmy to the rest of the company. His open, friendly face and complete lack of inhibition endeared him to most people at sight, but Matt's acknowledgement of his presence was cold enough to be described as frigid. He looked towards Nicola with raised eyebrows and she in return glared back at him for daring to be critical of one of her friends. Jimmy might have been guilty of high spirits in dancing her off her feet as he had, but that was no reason, she told herself, why Matt Devlin should treat him as if he were an inferior being. All the warm feelings of championship she was capable of swelled up inside her, on Jimmy's behalf, and as Matt looked on, she lifted her chin defiantly and slipped her hand through Jimmy's arm with every indication of intimacy. Jimmy's eyes lit up with pleasure. He turned to the interested onlookers and asked :

'Do any of you know a good place around here where I can take my best girl? Somewhere we can eat and maybe dance afterwards?'

Matt, for some reason Nicola could not fathom, looked intensely annoyed. The friendly smile that had been of such short duration had faded from his lips and her heart sank as once more he turned a black-frowned countenance towards her. He seemed about to make an angry remark, but then his eyes flickered to where her arm still rested on Jimmy's. He cleared the frown from his face with an effort and spoke calmly. Every nerve in her body shrank in negation as he asked Jimmy, smooth as silk, if he would care to join himself and Aline. He raised his voice a little to reach Liz and the girls.

'Would you like me to provide you girls with escorts and then we could make up a party—I can assure you you'll enjoy it?'

The girls enthusiastically agreed to his plan and he excused himself in order to phone some of his friends who, he told them, would be more than delighted to partner them for the evening. Nicola was cold with horror. She tried to dissuade Jimmy from joining the party, but he pooh-poohed her suggestion that they should have a quiet supper at home.

'What's got into you, Nicola? You never used to be an advocate of quiet little supper parties, *à deux*, I think it must be a case of absence makes the heart grow fonder, eh?'

She forced her stiff lips to return his mischievous smile and chanced a look in Aline's direction. She was standing a little apart, looking bored and impatient. Her plan had backfired on her and she was making no effort to hide her chagrin. The thought of having to share Matt with a crowd of people, especially Nicola and her friends who constituted a threat to her peace of mind, glamour and excitement surrounding them as it did, was causing her no small anger.

She gave him a brilliant smile, however, when he returned from the manager's office where he had been phoning his friends, and hooked her arm possessively in his as he explained to the girls that his friends had unanimously agreed to his plan and that they would arrive, with their cars, in less than fifteen minutes.

Shortly afterwards, they were on their way. Nicola, ensconced with Jimmy in the back of the car provided by Liz's partner, was too hurt and miserable to respond to his chaffing. He attempted to put his arm around her, but she shrugged it off sharply. His quick look of hurt went unnoticed by Nicola, who was staring blankly out of the window as the long ribbon of road that stretched far into the hills was gobbled up by the speeding roadster.

He regarded her speculatively and let his arm fall to his knee.

'What's wrong, sweetheart? Tired?'

'No, it's not that, Jimmy. I'm just not in the mood.'

He took a cigarette from his case and as the glow from his lighter lit the blackness of the interior he raked her face with eyes that understood more than she realized.

'If you're so much in love with him that you can't bear any other man to touch you, why are you letting that female with a look of a hungry shark monopolize his company?'

She was speechless with surprise and mortification. Was it so obvious to everyone, she wondered, that she was in love with her boss? She turned away to hide the tears that had spurted to her eyes before she could will them away, but Jimmy wasn't going to let her off so easily. He took her face in his hands and made her look at him. Liz and her escort were busily engaged in getting to know each other, so she was spared their interest.

'You needn't worry, my love. It isn't obvious to everyone, as you're thinking, it's just that . . . being so much in love with you I'm sensitive to atmosphere. I couldn't help noticing the number of times your eyes turn towards him, the way you come to life when he speaks to you. And as for him . . . ! I swear I feel nervous every time he looks in my direction. The icy blast of his dislike has me frozen to the marrow!'

Nicola, despite herself, had to smile at this highly exaggerated statement, as he had intended she should. He patted her cheek and assured her gently:

'You need some kind of support, darling, I can sense it. And what's the use of having good old Jimmy at hand if you don't intend to make use of him? I'm not asking any questions. I just want you to know that if I can help in any way I'll be only too pleased to. Understood?'

She did not miss the slight bitterness in his voice as he derided himself to her. Her own unhappiness made her sympathetic towards a fellow sufferer. For two years he had been her constant shadow and a tower of strength to both Liz and herself, but she had made it known to him, very definitely, that she could offer no more than friendship. He clowned his way through life so much that they had been apt to forget he had deeper feelings, referring to him as 'old faithful' and so on, till they had forgotten completely that he had ever professed to love Nicola. He had been treated as part of the furnishings, and now Nicola was hating herself for the unthinking heartburning they must have caused him by treating him with less seriousness than he deserved. Her remorse put more warmth than she realized into her voice as she responded to him.

'Oh, Jimmy! I've been a heartless beast to you in the past, haven't I? I didn't know, you see, what it felt like to be in love. It's as if I've just wakened from a coma. The grass is suddenly so much greener; the sky bluer; the birds sing more sweetly, but only when I'm with him, Jimmy! And I'll never know that sort of beauty again, for I mustn't love him, and if I can't have him . . .' she looked apologetically at Jimmy, 'I don't want anyone!'

Jimmy flinched a little, then with cool aplomb assured her:

'If that's the way you feel, little Nicola, we shall have to see to it that you two have the opportunity to get together to iron out your difficulties. I'm not having my best girl weeping her heart out over a misunderstanding that could probably be put right with the help of five minutes alone in the moonlight.'

She tried to tell him: 'No! No, you don't understand. I don't want to be alone with him! I want you to stay by my side every minute.' But she was too late. The car had drawn up in front of the roadhouse and Jimmy and Liz were in the middle of an altercation about whether they should eat first and dance later, or vice versa.

By the time the car was parked they had been joined by the rest of the party; all but Matt and Aline, who had gone straight into the brilliantly lit bar on the ground floor of the new building. They voted unanimously to join them, so Nicola had no choice but to drag her reluctant feet in their wake. She had a feeling that the evening was going to be an utter fiasco. How, she asked herself, can I live through the evening watching Matt with Aline Royston by his side, clinging and triumphant? The sight of the two of them together was enough to cause jealous feelings she was appalled to find she possessed coursing through her. As for food, the very thought sickened her. She stood for a moment outside the doorway, in the blessed darkness, to compose herself before entering. Tonight she was going to be called upon to act as she had never had to act before. To pretend, before Aline's sharp eyes, an indifference she did not feel towards Matt. Either that, or be ridiculed in front of her friends, and him. The very thought was enough to square her shoulders and to lift her chin a fraction higher. Resolutely, she stepped through the door which, to her fevered imagination, led to a room that had already taken on the aspect of an arena.

CHAPTER XII

LIZ buttonholed her as soon as they reached the powder-room. They hadn't had one minute to themselves since she had arrived, and Nicola saw, by the light of battle in her eyes, that she was not going to be deterred from having the heart-to-heart talk she had been bursting for since she first set foot in Carswell.

'Nicola,' she began, 'if you don't tell me all about that adorable man I'll die of curiosity! Is *he* the beast?'

'Which man do you mean?' Nicola dissembled, her heart sinking to her shoes at the thought of Liz probing the wound that was already hurting more than she could bear. Liz gave her a long, thoughtful look. For the first time she noticed that her friend's eyes were dark with pain, her small face pointed and drawn as she fought to compose her trembling mouth to a deceiving, wavering smile. She drew in her breath with a sharp hiss and her voice was charged with compassion as she stood before Nicola and willed her to look at her.

'Which man . . .? The one you've fallen head over heels in love with, my dear! And don't deny it, because I would refuse to believe you. I've suffered the pangs too often myself not to be able to recognize it in others. Come now, Nicola, admit it!'

Nicola wanted to deny it, for she felt ashamed that her emotions should be so clearly written on her face for all to see—first Jimmy, and now Liz. But with her friend's kind eyes upon her face she found it impossible to lie. Gallantly she squared her shoulders and told her:

'Yes, Liz, I love him. But don't expect a happy-ever-after ending, for it's a very one-sided attraction and nothing can come of it.'

She knew she owed it to Liz to explain further, but felt she couldn't just then. In a few minutes she would have to face Matt in the company of Aline Royston; she needed to call upon all her reserves of strength to face that ordeal and she knew she couldn't do it unless she could make her mind a blank and her senses numb.

'Liz, I can't talk about it now . . . Later, when we're alone, I'll try to explain, but please leave it for the time being. I don't think,' her voice broke a little, 'I could get through the evening if I had to talk about it now!'

Liz could always be relied upon to understand. She gave Nicola's arm a tight squeeze, but said nothing. Nicola smiled back gratefully, a rather woebegone smile that touched Liz's heart with its valour. She didn't need an explanation, for the situation was as old as nature, she told herself. There was a serpent in the garden to throw a spanner in the works; rather a mixed metaphor, but it explained things to Liz's satisfaction, or rather, to her dissatisfaction. Aline's name immediately sprang into her mind. She knew, of course, that there was more between Matt and Nicola than Aline Royston, but, to her over-simplified mind, to get rid of the serpent would leave the way open for minorities to resolve themselves. Nicola, mercifully unaware of the scheme hatching under her friend's placid brow, led the way into the bar.

The Huntsman, a very popular new venue of the more sophisticated set, was almost empty. It being mid-week and rather early in the season they had the place practically to themselves, so they were able to spread around the bar without fear of disturbing other customers. Nicola and Liz joined Jimmy and Liz's escort, a young man named Derek, who was already showing signs of infatuation with Liz and had the air of hardly being able to

believe his luck at having the good fortune to partner
such a gorgeous creature. Matt and Aline Royston were
having an earnest discussion with the manager, obviously
an acquaintance of Matt's, for he was sitting at their
table laughing at something he had said. Nicola turned
her chair so as to avoid looking in their direction and
when Jimmy started his usual clowning her laughter
could be heard ringing out above the noise of the general
hum of conversation. Encouraged, Jimmy excelled himself. His companions were treated to a repertoire of
jokes and anecdotes that had them helpless with laughter
and, consequently, gathered the rest of the company
around their table to join in the fun. All except Matt
and Aline Royston. Whether from politeness to the
manager, or from inclination, they stayed where they
were at the far end of the room.

The position changed, however, when the soft-footed
Italian head waiter informed them that their table was
ready. Matt, being the host, sat at the head with Aline
at his right and the others seated themselves haphazardly
in the first chairs they came to. Nicola led the way
determinedly to the foot of the table, as far away from
Matt as possible, and out of sight of his dark, grave face.
All through the meal she chattered and laughed as
Jimmy continued to entertain everyone within earshot,
but she was aware every minute of the suave attention
Matt paid to his guests as he tendered solicitously to their
needs. She dared a look, once, when she knew his attention was occupied by a waiter, and was confused and
sickened by the look of malevolence that reached down
the table from Aline Royston's hard, diamond-bright
eyes. She hurriedly dropped her eyes to her plate, but
the sight of the food nauseated her so much that she
pushed her plate away with a shudder of distaste. After
the meal, when almost everyone was in a state of good-
humoured repletion the sound of musicians tuning up

drew them from the warmth and comfort of the dining-room towards a large room with small tables and chairs set around a space of a comfortably adequate size for dancing. At the far end of the room was a dais holding a piano, drums, and microphone. Four musicians comprised the band which swung into a contagious samba as soon as the first of the party reached the floor. No one needed urging to join in, least of all Jimmy; he swept Nicola on to the floor with a whoop of delight that reached Matt, who was just leaving the dining-room with Aline Royston. He frowned his distaste, and Aline, quick to take advantage of his show of displeasure, pressed home her advantage. With a look of disdain underlining her query she asked:

'Really, Matt! Do we have to join in this ridiculous display? I'm quite certain that young man has had too much to drink and I don't care to be associated with him. I must say your secretary isn't what one might call *choosy* about her admirers, don't you agree?'

She waited with narrowed eyes for him to confirm her opinion, but his impassive expression gave nothing away; his countenance, if anything, was grimmer than ever. She gave a moue of impatience. He really was being a drag this evening. All through dinner he had maintained a tight-lipped courtesy to everyone around him, but she was aware, from the very fact that his eyes had not once wavered in the direction of Nicola and her friends, that his mind was preoccupied with thoughts of her. She clenched her teeth with impotent rage, then willed a charming smile to her lips. He obviously had no intention of leaving, for he was guiding her purposely towards the laughing revellers on the dance floor. It behoved her, if she couldn't get him to herself, to make it quite clear to the others that she had prior claim to his attention.

Nicola, dancing past in Jimmy's arms, felt a stab of primitive jealousy that horrified her as she witnessed Aline melt against Matt, her smooth rounded arm clinging to his broad black-clad shoulder, her perfect white teeth showing between parted, seductive lips in a smile of satisfaction as he inclined his head towards her while they moved together in time to the music. Quickly, she averted her head, but not before Aline had seen her. Jimmy began showing off by introducing some special steps of his own that taxed her ability to the limit, so even if she had wanted to she could not risk another quick glance in Matt's direction. She tortured herself by picturing them together, seemingly engrossed, and could not dispel from her mind the overwhelming triumph that had snaked from Aline Royston when their eyes had met.

Nicola's friends believed in working hard and playing harder; the fun raged fast and furious with the girls changing partners for every dance and communicating their gay, uninhibited love of life to their more sedate partners whose environment, more than their inclinations, was responsible for their more sober attitude to life. Matt's friends, as a rule, had to consider the effect their behaviour might have on their rather hidebound families and business acquaintances and their approach to enjoyment was therefore more circumspect. But this evening, in the company of girls used to being fêted by men of the world with all the wonders of the capital city with which to woo them, they forgot to be models of north-country businessmen, sober and industrious scions of Carswell, and remembered only that they were young and eager; each congratulating himself on his good fortune to be holding a bundle of infectious charm by the waist; each wishing that the night would last for ever.

By eleven o'clock the gathering had reached an almost carnival atmosphere. Even Aline had softened enough to accept graciously Jimmy's offer to teach her some of his more intricate dance steps and was led on to the floor before realizing that she had left Matt sitting at the table with only Liz and Nicola for company. She hesitated for a moment as if she would go back, but Jimmy summed up the situation with his usual perspicacity and twinkled the length of the floor with her before she could find words to protest. Matt had danced with each girl in turn, shedding his rather grave manner completely as their effervescent spirits chased his earlier sternness as easily as the sun's first rays disperse a delicate frost. They had flirted with him outrageously, thereby stamping their own brand of unqualified approval on him as a host, and welcoming him into their close circle as a friend of Nicola's. He had not approached Nicola to partner him, and as the evening progressed her heart grew heavy with the knowledge that he was deliberately avoiding her.

Now, as Derek claimed Liz, her pulses leapt. She and Matt were the only two who were not dancing, if he ignored her now his action would be obvious to everyone. She forced herself to look across the table in his direction. He was watching her, his look cool and calculating, the smiles he reserved for her friends conspicuous by their absence. Chilled to the bone, she could merely nod in answer to the question, asked with sardonic humour, 'May I have the pleasure, Nicola?'

He held her loosely at first, as if averse to her nearness, but as he had on two occasions to draw her nearer in order to avoid a collision, they found themselves, almost without volition, dancing closely together with her head just on level with his shoulder and his breath fanning her brow. The lights were lowered and the band began softly playing the traditional last waltz. Nicola felt the tension was becoming unbearable as they circled the room without speaking. She was unable to relax; his firm hand on her waist felt like an iron band and her breath fluttered in her throat like the beating of hundreds of tiny wings. At last the music stopped and the lights blazed on, for the playing of the National Anthem. The sudden switch from darkness to light brought blessed relief. She sped from his side before he could offer the conventional thanks and could not resist a desperate back-glance as she ran. He was looking after her, an enig-matic look on his face. But she didn't care that her swift flight must have indicated an aversion to his near-ness. All she wanted was release from the insufferable strain of his company and a moment of solitude in which to marshal her scattered emotions.

Liz, meanwhile, was stalking Jimmy with a view to seeking his co-operation. She found him standing out-side, moodily smoking a cigarette while he waited for Derek to bring the car to the front entrance. His usual sunny smile was missing when he turned at the sound of her voice, but he tried to deceive her by turning on a gaiety that, sadly, had a superficial, hollow ring. Liz's heart smote her for what she was about to ask of him. She had no doubt he had joined their party with the sole object of meeting Nicola and perhaps persuading her to consider him more seriously than she had in the past; his present despondency was proof enough that he had recognized the futility of pursuing such a course. Not-withstanding this, Liz did not waver in her intention. She touched his sleeve with a sympathetic hand, convey-ing without the need of words her understanding of his mood, then with a swift look round to make sure she could not be overheard, she began :

'Jimmy, I need your help !'

His disinterested, 'Oh, yes?' showed his thoughts were still occupied elsewhere. She tried again.

'*Nicola* needs your help !'

He was all ears. Sure of his complete attention, Liz explained.

'She doesn't know what I'm asking you to do, Jimmy, and she'll probably be as mad as a bear when she finds out, but we must manage it so that she and Matt have some time together—without Aline Royston hovering in the background—so that they can come to terms with each other. Will you help me to get Aline out of the way so that Matt will have to drive Nicola home?'

For a minute she thought he was going to refuse, and she couldn't have found it in her heart to blame him if he had. His lips twisted in a smile of grotesque humour when, after wrestling with his conscience, he bowed to the inevitable and asked her :

'What sort of plan do you have in mind?'

This stopped Liz in her tracks, for she hadn't got round to planning out in detail the method she would use to entice Aline from Matt's side, and for the life of her she couldn't think of a way. She looked helplessly at Jimmy, who gave a snort of exasperation.

'Honestly, Liz, you're the giddy limit! You don't want my help, you want me to plan the whole blamed incident!'

This was an occasion when she thought it politic to use her wiles. Looking up at him with absolute confidence shining from her tranquil eyes, she admitted:

'I know I can rely on you, Jimmy. You're always full of bright ideas and they *always* work. Be a doll and see what you can dream up. Nicola's happiness depends upon it!'

He didn't reply to this in words, but shrugged his shoulders and indicated that he was completely stumped. Then, just as Derek drew his car up to the front entrance with a flourish, he saw Aline step out on to the courtyard and he hissed at Liz:

'We haven't time to plan, Liz, here she comes! Just play along with me and keep your fingers crossed!'

He left Liz to greet Aline with exaggerated exuberance.

'Aline, my sweet, I thought you were never coming!' He grabbed hold of her arm and bustled her towards the car door which Derek was thoughtfully holding open for Liz. Aline had no time to lodge much of a protest, sheer surprise robbed her of words, but she instinctively resisted Jimmy's efforts to propel her to the car.

'Take your hands off me! How dare you speak to me like that!'

She had found her voice at last. Jimmy blanched with comical dismay, but did not forget to urge her still closer to the open car. He looked round for Liz, a desperate plea in his eyes, and she responded at once.

'Oh, Aline,' she admonished, tongue in cheek, 'I'm astonished at the way you've managed to capture our Jimmy's heart in the short time he's known you! You really must let me into your secret. The poor man is desperate for your company, my dear. Surely you won't deny him it when you know he'll be going back to London tomorrow?'

This little altercation was strictly for the benefit of the other few members of the party who were standing listening with amusement, and it served to cover up the fact that Aline was still being propelled forward by Jimmy, who had a grasp on her arm that she could not break. With a final outrageous gesture, Jimmy stopped the angry words Aline was about to give voice to with an enthusiastic kiss, at the same time giving her a determined push that deposited her inside the car. He jumped in beside her while Liz rapidly banged the door shut and implored Derek, an amazed bystander, to 'step on it, for the love of heaven!'

Derek followed her instructions to the letter and sent the car hurtling along the road and out of sight before anyone could see Aline's face, contorted with fury, at the back window.

Nicola was the last out of the cloakroom. She had been looking for Liz for the better part of ten minutes and was puzzled because there was no sign of her anywhere. She had asked the other girls as one by one they had left with their escorts, but they had all confessed ignorance of her whereabouts. She stepped outside thinking to find Jimmy and was amazed to see the forecourt empty, but for one car. The change from the brilliantly-lit interior of the roadhouse to the inky blackness of the night blinded her for an instant. She focused her eyes on the solitary car and could just make out the figure of a man leaning against the bonnet in an obviously waiting attitude. He sent the cigarette he was smoking spinning from his hand to land with a sharp hiss in a puddle a few yards away, then he straightened up and began walking towards her. He had walked only a few paces when she realized it was Matt. Panic caught at her throat. For a moment she was tempted to flee back into the haven of light behind her. All through the evening she had longed to escape the noisy, ostentatious atmosphere within, but now, as Matt's tall figure advanced towards her, it appeared to her fevered imagination as an oasis of calm and safety. He reached her side and gave a grim smile as he noted her slim figure tensed and poised as if for flight. In the darkness his bulk loomed over her, tall and forbidding, his voice, when he spoke, was clipped and stern.

'It seems we're the only two left here. If you're ready we'll go.'

She looked around, fervently willing someone to appear from out of the darkness to rescue her from the ordeal of a solitary drive through the darkness with Matt, a cold stranger who could have offered a lift to a hitchhiker with more cordiality.

'Where's Liz and Jimmy?' she gasped out.

'I was informed that they drove off with Aline in Derek's car a good ten minutes ago. A strange thing to happen, all things considered, but,' he shrugged as if impatient to be on his way, 'we won't find out anything standing here. I'm afraid that, like it or not, you'll have to put up with me as an escort.'

Numbly, she followed him to the car and slid into the seat next to his. As he started the engine the moon, an enormous full, golden disc, sailed from behind ridges of heavily banked clouds to illuminate the ribbon of road in front of them with an eerie brightness. Nicola shuddered, for some unknown reason, and crouched down in her seat, pulling the collar of her coat closer up to her chin. He gave her a negligent glance and asked if she were cold.

'No . . . not really,' she stammered. 'I'll be all right in a minute when the heater gets warmed up.'

He nodded his head slightly in agreement and they lapsed into a silence that lasted until they reached the outskirts of Carswell. It was a brooding, waiting silence, so pregnant with feeling that Nicola felt a hysterical need to scream or cry out in order to break the stultifying pressure on her nerves. Thankfully, she watched the familiar landmarks slide past as the car entered the city and negotiated the empty streets as he drove towards her home. She expelled her breath gratefully when he slowed down to turn the corner that led to her aunt's house, but checked it with alarm when, instead of turning into the drive, he slewed to the left and ran the car down a narrow path that led to the river's edge. He brought it to a standstill in the shadow of a high, grassy bank, a favourite spot for courting couples, and turned to regard her tense, questioning eyes with a grim, purposeful look.

Her voice was a small thread of sound when she whispered:

'Why have you stopped here?'

He didn't answer immediately, but took out his cigarette case and offered it to her. She waved it away, impatient for him to get on with what he had to say, so she could leave him to gain the beckoning safety of the house. She heard the blood pounding in her ears as she waited, then realized that the noise she could hear came from the flood-swollen waterfall that was hurling tons of water into the dam. The moon came out from behind a cloud to give a cold, menacing look to the frothing, angry water, and she shivered and clutched her wrap closer around her. He was quick to notice this, and asked her, 'Are you still cold?' while at the same time putting his arm around her shoulders to adjust the collar of her wrap to give her more warmth. She nervously jerked away from his hand and looked up at him with frightened eyes. In the dimness of the car she could hardly make out his features, but she felt him stiffen at her instinctive repulsion. He stubbed out his cigarette and whipped out viciously:

'It's all right, Nicola, I'm not going to force my unwelcome attentions upon you yet again! I don't know why, but you seem to have an absolutely wrong conception of my character. It's the first time in my life that I've had a woman *afraid* of me, and it's a most unpleasant sensation.'

Her voice was shaking when she answered:

'Why have you brought me here? Why couldn't you just have driven me to the house?'

He became completely still, and then told her:

'I want to apologize to you for my past behaviour!'

Her voice incredulous, she repeated: 'Apologize? You...?'

Her tone angered him. He slewed round to face her and bit out :

'Yes, apologize! I'm not above that, you know, if I think I've wronged someone,' he stressed his next words. 'Incredible as it may seem to you, I do have *some* good points!'

'What . . . what has made you decide only this evening that you owe me an apology,' she stuttered, 'why not on an earlier occasion? There have been plenty,' she added with bitterness.

He waited for a while, then, ignoring her question, he asked her another :

'This . . . Jimmy Sorenson. Is he an old friend?'

She answered without hesitation. 'Yes, a *very* old friend.'

Very slowly and distinctly, he questioned her again:

'Do you love him?'

She wanted to seize upon Jimmy as her salvation, her shield behind which she could shelter from his probing questions and from her speculative acquaintances in the works. If she announced her engagement to Jimmy the rumours that were rife would be scotched and she would perhaps be able to lift her head again. But she knew that such a course would be unfair to Jimmy, he was too nice a person to be used and then discarded when he was no longer wanted. But then, as she opened her mouth to tell Matt that Jimmy was a dear friend, and no more, she was horrified to hear her own voice saying with conviction:

'Yes, I love him very much.'

Her words dropped into the silence before she could call them back and she lifted her hand to her mouth with a gasp of dismay. She waited for Matt's reaction and winced as she heard him say with cold disinterest:

'Then I must offer my best wishes to you both.'

Suddenly he seemed to think there was no more to be said, for he switched on the engine and began reversing the car prior to driving it up to the front of her aunt's house. He jerked out a stern 'good-night' and drove away without realizing that, in her misery, she was incapable of answering him.

She crept up to her room, her heart heavy, and prepared herself for bed, but not to sleep. She knew that she had a decision to make, one that would take all of what was left of the night to resolve.

CHAPTER XIII

CHARLES DEVLIN had insisted that Nicola should stay away from the office on the morning after the show so as to have a few hours with her friends before they left for London. This she had willingly agreed to do, for she knew that Liz would welcome the chance to catch up on all that had happened since her arrival in her home town and the events that had led to her employment at Scaur Bank Mills.

But as she waited, heavy-eyed, in her aunt's drawing-room for her arrival she knew, finally and absolutely, that after last night she could never go back to work for Matt again, no matter what repercussions her decision might cause. She forced her mind away from her dishonesty of the previous night and the subsequent agony of mind which was responsible for the black circles underlining the wretchedness in her eyes. Her fingers entwined themselves round a cord that hung from the heavy brocade curtains at the window and plucked nervously at its frayed edge as she waited expectantly for the sight of Charles Devlin's car which was to bring Liz on a flying visit and also to pick up Jimmy and his luggage before they all left for the station. She wondered at Jimmy's absence. When she had gone down to breakfast that morning Sarah had informed her that he had had his early and had left word that he was going for a long walk and would be back in time to leave with Liz. He had taken a delighted Rufus with him—far from being a one-owner dog who pledged his allegiance only to his master, or in his case, mistress, Rufus made joyful friends with anyone who was energetic enough to take him for a tramp—and Jimmy seemed to find consolation in his fawning attentions.

Nicola was pleased that Sarah was out shopping and would not be present when Liz arrived. There was a guarded reticence between the two that worried her when she had time to think about it, and she wanted nothing disturbing to mar their leavetaking—a leavetaking that was to be merely a short prelude to her own departure from Carswell and the blissful anonymity of London where friends were content to live their lives and to let others live theirs without poking and prying into the inner recesses of a heart that was too sore to be subjected any longer to the sort of assault that had been made upon it recently.

She gave a sigh of relief as she saw the car turn into the drive and ran to greet Liz who was just alighting from it as she opened the front door. Her friend's expectant smile faded abruptly when she was confronted, not with the radiant face of a girl whose world was all that was wonderful, but with a wan, pale countenance that was making mockery of the heroic smile wavering on her mobile mouth. She took a deep breath and tried to hide the dismay she felt at the sight of Nicola's obvious unhappiness.

'Good morning, love!' and then, tentatively, 'Did you get home all right last night?'

Liz's heart sank as she noted the flicker of pain her words evoked before she replied in a false, too-bright voice that didn't deceive her for a moment :

'Oh, yes, thank you, Liz. Matt brought me home. But where on earth did you get to? And Jimmy?'

They were walking towards the drawing-room while they were speaking and Liz busied herself getting rid of her coat and handbag before sitting down on the settee, and she patted the place next to her, invitingly, before replying. When Nicola had settled down beside her, she decided to be blunt and met her eyes unflinchingly as she told her calmly :

'We kidnapped Aline Royston so as to leave you a clear field with Matt. I haven't seen him this morning to find out how things went, but now that I've seen you I needn't ask. Our efforts were a pitiful waste of time, obviously.'

She waited imperturbably for Nicola's wrath to fall on her head, quite prepared to weather it in the cause of friendship, but there was so little fire in Nicola's response she knew that things had gone really desperately wrong.

'That was very silly of you both. I suppose you meant to be kind, so I should thank you, but I hope you'll excuse me if I don't !'

Liz sighed and put her hand on Nicola's arm.

'Want to tell me about it?'

'Not really,' was Nicola's rather bitter reply. 'But I suppose you're entitled to know the ending, seeing you were in on the beginning.' She proceeded to tell Liz, in a flat voice, all that had happened between her and Matt, beginning with their first meeting in the hut and finishing with tell-tale brevity at their abrupt parting the evening before. When she finished, Liz was bursting with indignation and didn't hesitate to communicate her thoughts to Nicola.

'You're in love with Matt, deeply in love, yet you intend leaving him in ignorance of the true facts, without a chance to justify himself? Or of allowing his father to justify himself? How could you, Nicola ! You're being most unfair, to them and to yourself ! You have no right to keep them in ignorance of the things your aunt has charged them with, and you're a *fool* to allow Aline Royston a clear field with Matt. If you love him you ought to be prepared to fight for him, not give in meekly as you are doing ! And I'll tell you something else, Nicola,' Liz was really angry now, 'I don't care what your Aunt Sarah has told you about the Devlins, I think they're two of the most charming men I've ever met in my life, and what's more, the way you're treating them, you don't deserve anyone's sympathy!'

Nicola flinched, but did not waver from her decision. Liz was hard put to check her temper when she told her:

'I'm going up to the office this afternoon to gather up my belongings and to give in my notice. I can't face the idea of working with Matt Devlin another day—indeed, I *won't* work with him!' Liz knew better than to argue with a tone of voice that was adamant in the extreme and was silent when Nicola went on:

'I'll be back in London next week, Liz. Dulcie can resolve her own problems, I've had enough!'

Liz recognized the near-hysteria in her last remark and bit back the words of condemnation that had risen to her lips. Somehow, some time, things would have to be put right between her and Matt, but at the moment Nicola needed a friend more than she had ever needed one in her life before, and Liz responded with aching sympathy as she recognized the call for help that was struggling to be heard under the brave defiance of her words.

'All right, darling. I'll tell Dulcie that you're leaving here and that she'll have to make other arrangements if she intends staying in London. When you come back I'll have the flat spick and span and we'll carry on as if this interlude in Carswell had never been. Promise me you won't worry yourself sick about that aunt of yours, and that you'll stick to your guns when she finds out about your leaving here? No more knuckling under to emotional blackmail, remember!'

'I promise, Liz. This time,' and Liz knew she meant it, 'I'm going to do what *I* want, and if Aunt Sarah doesn't like it it'll be just too bad!'

Jimmy chose that moment to return with Rufus and the opportunity for more discussion was lost. As he entered the room his eyes immediately slewed to Nicola, expecting, as Liz had, to see a radiant look of happiness, but he turned a puzzled look on Liz when, once again Nicola's acting proved to be lacking in sincerity before the eyes of someone who loved her. He ached to ask why her eyes had lost their sparkle and her face the merry expression he was so used to seeing there, but was warned by a cautioning shake of the head from Liz to say nothing. He contained his soul in patience until Liz could provide the answers to the questions he was clamouring to ask and, instead, adopted the attitude of a man dying of thirst. With his hands clutching his throat and his tongue lolling from his mouth, he beseeched her :

'Coffee! Coffee, for the love of Allah! Any chance of a cup of coffee for a thirsty man?'

Their laughter cleared the air of tension, and as Nicola made her way to the kitchen to oblige him with the sought-for drink, Liz whispered to him fiercely :

'Not a word about last night! Everything went wrong and they're at even worse loggerheads than they were before we decided to interfere. I'll tell you more on the train, but I can gladden your heart by telling you that she's coming back to London for good, next week . . . Ssh, she's coming back!'

The last bit of news cheered Jimmy immensely, so much so that he made the rest of the time before they had to leave for the station hilarious with his clowning and rapier wit. If Nicola's laughter was cloaking heartache it at least had the effect of lightening the burden of her thoughts for a little while, and Jimmy felt his effort was well worth it when he saw her gratefully relax and smile with her eyes as well as with her lips. All too soon, it seemed to her, the car was back for them. As she stood on the step waving goodbye her lightheartedness slid from her with every revolution of the car's wheels, till, when it was out of sight, a wave of despondency washed over her, creating a lump in her throat and a tightness at the corners of her mouth as she compressed her lips firmly to suppress their quivering. The ordeal in front of her again loomed large on the horizon—to tell the Devlins that she would no longer be working for them, to meet Matt's eyes and have to pretend indifference to the cold impersonality in their depths, to ignore Charles Devlin's puzzled regard and watch the kindly interest change to hurt dignity, as it was bound to, when she offered no explanation of her decision to leave the mill and everyone connected with it, and return to London. Suddenly, the idea of waiting and brooding over the action that had to be taken was abhorrent to her. She wouldn't wait until the afternoon to face them, she decided, she would go this morning and get it over with.

Once the decision was made she didn't hesitate to carry it out. She raced upstairs to change, for she needed something morale-boosting to help in small measure to keep her equilibrium, and ran an impatient hand across the rail of outfits in her wardrobe. She pulled out one or two before deciding on a very formal suit of such a deep shade of grey as to be almost black. Normally, she would not have dreamed of wearing it to the office, for the material was expensive and the style far too sophisticated for an ordinary working day. But this was not an ordinary day, she told herself, and she would not be working when she got to the Mill, merely talking her way out of a job and out of the lives of the men who employed her. For this final break she needed something stunning to stiffen her morale, and as she looked into the mirror and saw how perfectly her figure was outlined by the superb lines of the suit, and how well the matt white of the blouse that went with it projected the translucent glow of her skin and acted as a foil for the vivid beauty of her hair, she was well satisfied. She might well have to face scorn and questioning in the following hour, but she intended leaving the owners of Scaur Bank Mills with a picture of cool dignity to remember her by.

She reached the office just in time to share a cup of coffee with Jessica, who was full of admiration of the way in which Nicola had managed the show and of her model friends. Her dismay at the news that she was leaving for London was slightly eased by Nicola's promise to send her all the information she would require to further her plan to become a model, and she was blissfully dreaming dreams in that direction when Nicola, after eliciting the information that Matt was in his office, braced herself and walked through into the inner room.

He looked up inquiringly when she entered, having already been told not to expect her until the following day, and watched with narrowed eyes while she made her way towards his desk. Her heart was thumping madly, but she willed herself not to show it. She stopped a few steps away from him and met the undisguised coldness in his eyes with a proud lift of her fiery head. She saw he had no intention of easing the strain of their meeting by speaking first, so she jerked out :

'I've come to give in my notice. I shall be returning to London next week, but I'd like to leave immediately, if possible.'

A nerve flickered at the corner of his mouth as she waited for his reaction to the bald statement. When she thought he was never going to answer, his voice cut into the silence in a frozen monotone:

'Very well, Miss Brent. If that is what you wish, naturally I won't stand in your way.'

He stood up and walked round the desk until he was within a few feet of her. She met his bleak look without showing how the cold, punctilious 'Miss Brent' had hurt her after having heard him call her Nicola for even such a short time. He held out his hand.

'It only remains for us to say goodbye with what grace we can muster, doesn't it?'

She put the tips of her fingers on his to acknowledge the truth of his statement, but before she could answer, the door was opened to admit Charles Devlin and Edith, followed by Aline Royston.

To onlookers, the guilty start she gave as she pulled her hand away from Matt's might have been construed as a modest attempt to hide the fact that they had been holding hands. Aline Royston's hard eyes glittered dangerously as a slow tide of very becoming colour swept Nicola's face. Charles gave vent to a delighted exclamation when he saw her and hurried to her side with unconcealed pleasure.

'Nicola, my dear! This is very naughty of you! I thought I told you to take the day off?'

The combination of finding her alone with Matt and now Charles's show of intimacy made Aline mad enough to chance throwing into the conversation a piece of information she had picked up the evening before from Jimmy, who had unknowingly put a weapon in her hands. She was unsure of its value, but was hoping to discredit Nicola in some way when she said meaningly:

'I'm surprised at you, Miss Brent. I would have thought you would have taken the opportunity of helping your *Aunt Sarah* with her housework!'

Matt seemed the only one undisturbed by the remark. Charles gave a visible start and looked straight at Nicola, who was the picture of confusion, while Edith seemed hardly to be able to credit that she had heard aright. Aline drawled hatefully, sure now that she had dropped a bombshell:

'Well, Miss Brent, aren't you going to tell us why you pretended to be staying with Sarah Dawson only temporarily while all the time covering up the fact that you are her niece *and Dulcie Dawson's cousin?*'

This drew Matt's startled attention. The mention of his late secretary's name seemed to embarrass him rather, because he reddened slightly before asking Nicola:

'Is that the reason you asked for information about Dulcie? But surely her mother could have told you all you wanted to know? Oh, but perhaps not. . .!'

For the first time in their acquaintance, Matt was out of countenance. Nicola was puzzled by his reaction, and a little sickened by his ill-at-ease, guilty look. She was suddenly ashamed of the doubts she had been harbouring about the validity of her aunt's and Dulcie's statements, and it was anger at herself that made her voice sharp when she challenged him.

'No. Mr. Devlin, her mother couldn't tell me anything. That's why I threw up my job in London. I came to Carswell to find out why she had been dismissed from your service without a reference, and for no apparent reason other than a sudden caprice on your part. But then,' she added bitterly, 'my family have all, at one time or another, been victims of your family's caprice!'

If this remark puzzled Matt it seemed to clarify something for Charles, for he pushed past his nephew to stand before Nicola with dawning wonder in his eyes.

He seemed to search her face for something and, when she turned on him, her eyes now flashing beacons of fury, he seemed satisfied, for he smiled away her antagonism and put his hands on her shoulders.

'Marcia's daughter. . .!' he murmured softly. 'Marcia's daughter, without a doubt!'

The seeming hypocrisy of the almost worshipful way he spoke her mother's name goaded Nicola beyond endurance.

'Yes! Marcia Brent was my mother, and you killed her, and my father too!'

After horrified gasps from Aline and Edith, and a muttered imprecation from Matt, the room seemed filled with a dreadful silence. Charles's face whitened, and he took a step back as her challenge echoed round the room.

'My dear. . . . !' He seemed incapable of finding words to refute the dreadful charge she laid before him. Matt stepped in with a stern warning.

'I think you'd better clarify that statement, Nicola.' The moment was too fraught with emotion for him to remember to be formal, but the whiplash in his voice was unmistakable and goaded Nicola even further.

'I don't need to clarify it,' the searing resentment of years of injustice was now out in the open and she was glad to confront them with it, 'my aunt has told me all about the despicable way he treated my parents. And you've shown yourself equally heartless by dismissing my cousin for no reason whatever!' Before Matt could retaliate, Aline broke in with a drawl of evident enjoyment :

'Oh, tell her, Matt, for heaven's sake! Tell her how her beloved cousin made your life impossible with her simpering attentions. How embarrassed you were when she insisted upon reading a *grande passion* into every kind gesture you made towards her and then, finally, when she realized it was no go, how she blatantly threw herself at your head, weeping, until you had to call for me to calm her down and to explain in words of one syllable that you simply weren't interested !'

The embarrassed colour Nicola had noted earlier when Dulcie's name had first been mentioned was now more in evidence than ever under Matt's tanned skin. That, combined with his silent discomfiture, convinced her that Aline was telling the truth, and her blood ran cold at the thought of the accusation she had hurled at him. Aline savoured every minute of Nicola's appalled silence and swift loss of colour, her triumphant stare drilled into Nicola's very heart as she watched her seek for reasons that might justify Dulcie's actions. Aline's triumph was

complete as she saw Nicola's shoulders sag with defeat
when she eventually acknowledged to herself that there
could be no possible justification for such actions. Her
eyes lifted to Matt's courageously.

'I seem to have been misinformed,' her voice was
stilted and chilled with resentment, 'on that count,' she
added defiantly, 'but I doubt if your father can explain
his actions as easily.'

Matt threw her a look of such scorn she all but winced.
'How can you believe such a thing of him? I don't
know the supposed circumstances of this *killing*, but even
so, I wouldn't believe it. Not in a hundred years!'

The combined force of their antagonism was a living
body directed against her. She looked round and saw
it reflected in Aline's face and again in Matt's. Edith was
regarding her with pitying sympathy tinged with dismay,
and only Charles Devlin seemed capable of viewing her
with anything approaching understanding. This, from
the man against whom all her hate had been directed,
was the last straw as far as Nicola was concerned. She
cared nothing whether her aunt had been wrong all these
years or whether Charles Devlin was an expert at covering up his baser emotions to give an impression of kindliness and good-heartedness. All she wanted was to be
away from the anger and censure that was surrounding
her, to leave the turmoil she had created behind her and
find a hole somewhere that she could crawl into to lick
her wounds. With the look of a chastened child, she
faced them and then turned and ran past the exultant
Aline, an impassive Matt, and a shocked and bewildered-
looking Edith.

Her flight seemed to bring Edith back to life. She
pulled herself together with a shake and thrust a condemning look at Aline as she sped past her to try to catch
Nicola before she was out of sight. Thankfully, she
caught sight of her and called her name with an urgency

that penetrated her frozen feelings. She waited passively until Edith had reached her side and then, with a longing to be proved right in her voice, and in her pleading face, she asked her :

'How could my aunt be wrong, all these years, Edith? Do you believe she could lie to me? Tell me it's Charles Devlin who is in the wrong! You know him better than anyone, so *tell me*. Is he as incapable as they all think of doing anyone a wrong?'

Edith took a deep breath. Somehow or other she had to prove to Nicola that Sarah Dawson was not to be trusted and that Charles Devlin, far from being the monster she thought he was, was the soul of honour.

'Tell me something, Nicola,' she asked on impulse. 'Do you think Matt is a villain? That he would be capable of harming anyone?'

She watched the fight for truth in Nicola's mind reflected in her green eyes and sighed thankfully when she turned to her and said simply :

'No, I don't think Matt would lie, even to save himself. I think I've always known it, but I can admit it now to myself for the first time. Is that sufficient answer, Edith?'

For the first time in her life, Edith was going to bare her soul to another human being and, habit being hard to break, she found it difficult to begin.

'You say that with such conviction, Nicola, because you're in love with Matt and you think you know him better because of it. You couldn't imagine yourself loving a man without finer qualities, therefore you're now certain in your own mind that Matt is a wonderful person. Isn't that so?'

'I suppose it is, Edith. The truth is so easy to find if only one looks hard enough for it.' Then she asked questioningly, 'but how does that effect Charles Devlin's character? Do you want me to believe that because I think Matt is good and honourable I should automatically assume his uncle to be the same?'

'Not exactly,' Edith smiled. 'I just want you to understand why I find it impossible to believe that Charles is any less wonderful than his nephew.   You see, my dear, I couldn't love a man who was less than he seemed to be, any more than you could!'

After her first initial perplexity Nicola understood.

'Oh, Edith! You mean *you* love Charles?'

'I've always loved him,' Edith admitted wryly, 'but the only woman who has ever held his heart is dead. Your mother, Nicola.   How could you believe that a man who loved your mother to distraction and who has cherished her memory all these years could ever harm her?   No, Nicola, your aunt was wrong about Matt, and I'm very much afraid she's misled you about Charles, too.'

Though stunned with shock, Nicola could not question the logic of this.   She put a hand to her throbbing head and whispered to Edith :

'Thank you for straightening me out, Edith.   I see now that I've been very foolish.'

With infinite pity, Edith asked her.

'Then what are you going to do about it, Nicola?'

Nicola squared her sagging shoulders and gave her a resolute look.   She looked to Edith, at that moment, tired out and completely beaten, but valiant enough to face her obligations squarely and with no lack of courage. Her answer brought a smile of satisfaction to Edith's face.

'I'm going somewhere quiet to sort out my thoughts, Edith.   And then ... *I'm going to find Aunt Sarah*!'

CHAPTER XIV

NICOLA found a spot on the river bank where she could sit, unobserved, to think about the problem she was faced with. After half an hour's cogitation she was no nearer to peace of mind than she had been when she fled from the office, so she dragged herself wearily to her feet and began making her way home with only one thing certain in her mind. She could decide nothing until she had confronted her aunt. All the way to the house she struggled with conflicting loyalties. One half of her mind violently rejected the thought that her aunt and cousin Dulcie could have cold-bloodedly deceived her. She could not accept that they would deliberately seek to turn her against the Devlins without a strong and valid reason. But the other treacherous half was whispering an insidious longing for it to be true. She would not allow herself to think of the effect it would have on her feelings if it should turn out that Sarah had lied. It would be an impossible situation, for, even if it did happen to be true, how could she go to Matt and tell him that she was agreeable to staying on now that she had discovered he was not the villain she had thought him to be? Neither he nor Charles would ever want to see her again after the dreadful accusations she had hurled at them both. She had to conclude that, whatever the outcome of her showdown with her aunt, it could make no difference to her plan to leave Carswell and return to London. Matt would have no use for a girl who had believed him, or his father, capable of the things she had accused them of.

Her footsteps quickened as she came within sight of

the house. Her aunt was certain to be home, since it was almost lunchtime and she was expecting her back for the meal. She entered the drive and was surprised to see the front door standing open. She walked straight through to the kitchen to look for her aunt, but although preparations for lunch were well under way, there was no sign of her. She retraced her steps and as she passed the drawing-room she heard a man's voice, a familiar voice, courteously refuse a proffered drink. Nicola stood frozen to immobility at the sheer unexpectedness of hearing Charles Devlin's voice, here, in her aunt's house. She listened deliberately as Sarah's voice prattled on, making conversation in a tone of pleased flattery. Why, Nicola thought with a mixture of amazement and disbelief, she's almost *fawning* over him!

Quite unashamedly she eavesdropped on their conversation. She heard Charles Devlin clear his throat before cutting through her aunt's chatter with a concise question.

'Sarah, would you mind telling me what tales you've been telling your niece about me?'

There was a moment's silence during which Nicola found herself digging her nails into her palms with tense concentration while she waited for the answer. She was dumbfounded to hear Sarah prevaricate apologetically :

'Oh, well, really, Charles . . .! I do hope you haven't been listening to Nicola's fantastic tales. The child has a vivid imagination that she carries into real life. She embarrasses me dreadfully at times!'

It was all of thirty seconds before Nicola's dazed mind could assimilate her aunt's words, and when she eventually did the force of her indignation almost choked her. With a crash, she sent the half-open door banging against its supports and entered the room with fury crackling from every pore.

'Aunt Sarah! How could you say such a thing! Why

don't you tell him what you told *me*? How he persecuted my mother and father because my mother wouldn't
marry him! How he was responsible for their having
to move from Carswell because he'd made my father's
life unbearable at the mill and of the fact that if he had
left them alone they wouldn't have been in the motor
accident that killed them both!' She turned to Charles
and cried angrily:

'That's what she told me! Now you tell me what
really happened!'

Charles swung round to an ashen-faced Sarah with
patent horror written on his face. His reaction was too
swiftly genuine to leave any doubt of his innocence, and
if any proof were needed that Sarah had lied, it was
written in large letters of guilt on her contorted features.
Nicola's dramatic entrance and the knowledge that she
must have heard her disclaimer of any knowledge of the
tales she had instilled into her since childhood had caught
her unawares and without time to fabricate any further
lies to cover up her deceit. With a feeling of sickening
unreality, Nicola saw her face mirror hate, fury, then a
vindictive jealousy that seemed to overwhelm reason and
cause her to throw caution to the winds. She backed
away from them like an enraged wildcat and spat out:

'All right, so I did tell her all those tales, and just like
her gullible mother she believed them! All my life I've
taken a back seat to the Brent family, and if I've managed to pay them back for it then I'm glad—*glad*, do you
hear?'

Nicola drew back from the frightening spectacle of a
woman almost berserk, but Charles seemed fascinated,
for he moved forward and urged her quietly:

'Yes, Sarah, go on. How did you take a back seat to
the Brents, and how did you deceive Marcia?'

Sarah gave a cracked sound of maniacal laughter.
Her eyes glittering with enjoyment, she answered him:

'Oh, you would like to know, wouldn't you, Charles? And I'll enjoy telling you now that I know your life has been ruined as you once ruined mine!'

At Charles's wave of refution, she began a spate of hysterical vituperation.

'Don't try to deny that you would have married me if Marcia hadn't come along to spoil things! You loved me first, I know you did, but I don't cast off as easily as you think, Charles Devlin. I made up my mind that if I couldn't have you then she wouldn't either! You remember, Charles, that time when you had to go abroad for a month and came back to find Marcia married to Alan Brent? You were heartbroken, weren't you? You couldn't understand why she'd married someone else when she'd promised to be your wife. But I know, Charles! Because, fool that she was, she believed me when I told her that by all moral right you ought to have been marrying me!'

Nicola thought Charles Devlin was going to strike Sarah. His face had gone grey and drawn as he listened to Sarah tell with sadistic enjoyment how she had ruined the only real romance in his life, and now he was looking at her as if the only way in which he could relieve the heartbreak she had aroused was to resort to physical violence, to smash her to the ground as she had smashed his hopes, so many years ago.

She could hardly bear to look at Sarah. Her words had shocked her beyond belief and she was still reeling under the blow of seeing her aunt in her true colours for the first time. She made a pitiful effort to speak to her, but the words ended in a meaningless croak. Sarah sensed rather than heard her strangled effort and rounded on her.

'And as for you! All these years I've had you as a constant reminder of the woman I hated! But I've put a spoke in your wheel as well, my lady. Don't think I haven't heard about you and Matt Devlin! You won't have any more luck than your mother did with the Devlins, because when he spurned Dulcie I made it my business to turn you against him, and I succeeded, didn't I, Nicola? History has repeated itself, for things are so bad between you now that he'll never marry you. And it serves you both right!'

Charles's voice halted her tirade. He was looking at her as if she were a loathsome reptile that had crawled from under his foot. Sarah was almost unrecognizable, for the spate of hate she was indulging in seemed to have deranged her mind. Her hands were clutching convulsively at her skirt and her eyes, set in a face burning with high colour, were furtively darting from Charles and then to Nicola with animal-like cunning.

'I think you're the most despicable creature it has ever been my misfortune to encounter,' Charles enunciated slowly and clearly, 'and as for ever contemplating marriage with you . . .! You may have thought I had some regard for you at one time, Sarah, but even in those days the only feeling you aroused in me was one of revulsion. I think, subconsciously, I sensed the twisted mentality you've shown today!' His voice dropped with unutterable weariness. 'My poor woman! You've hurt yourself far more than you've hurt any of us.'

Pity, from the man she had wronged so badly, was the last thing Sarah had expected. She looked at him for a short while as if unable to realize her defeat, then, her face working in a horrible grimace, she fell to the ground to lie in a crumpled heap at his feet. Nicola gave a half-strangled scream and ran towards her aunt's inert figure. But Charles, recognizing her symptoms, moved swiftly towards the telephone to call for a doctor.

Later, when they had taken Sarah's limp body away in an ambulance, he came back to the drawing-room where Nicola was sitting, dazed and immobile with shock.

He took hold of her cold, lifeless hand and began massaging the life back into it. She looked at him uncomprehendingly as he spoke her name, but drank obediently from the glass he held to her lips. The fiery liquid coursed through her veins and stirred her senses. His heart twisted with pity at the words she whispered in her bewilderment.

'She hated me. All these years I've loved her and thought she loved me, but she didn't. She hated me . . . !'

Her sorrow-filled eyes begged him to contradict her, but he could only comfort her by replying :

'She's sick, Nicola. It's been building up in her for years. That's what I meant when I said she had hurt herself far more than she hurt me, you, or your mother. Pity her, my dear, she's paying dearly for the wrong she did.'

'But how . . . why did she do what she did? What reason could she have for all that hatred she's stored up inside her all these years?'

Charles shook his head sadly. 'I can't find excuses for her, Nicola. But perhaps Shakespeare's words explained more than I can ever hope to, when he said, "The sweetest love changing its property turns to the sourest and most deadly hate". That, perhaps, is what happened in your aunt's case—and, my God, how she has made us all suffer for it !'

Nicola gave a shudder that moved Charles to action. He picked up the phone and asked to speak to Edith Stern. After a few terse sentences, he put it down and told Nicola:

'Come along, child, I want you to pack a few things. Edith is coming round in a few minutes to take you to her flat. You're not staying in this house another minute !'

Edith organized everything. She gathered together a few of Nicola's clothes and put them in a suitcase. Then she went round the house, checking that everything was left in order. She turned off the heat under the lunch they had not been fated to eat, and disposed of the contents of the pans. Then, satisfied that nothing important had been missed, she went back to join Nicola and Charles in the drawing-room. She put her arm around a still dazed Nicola and began urging her towards the door, outside which her car was waiting to take them back to her flat. Before she left, Nicola turned a beseeching look upon Charles and asked him huskily:

'Will you go to the hospital?'

Charles patted her on the shoulder. 'I'm going there immediately I see you off these premises, my dear. And I'll stay as long as I'm needed. I promise to send for you immediately she asks for you. And I'm quite certain,' he patted her shoulder kindly, 'that you'll be the first person she'll want beside her when she recovers. Now, go with Edith and try not to think of Sarah as you saw her a short while ago. Remember she is a very sick woman, Nicola, and is not responsible for anything she said.'

Nicola was glad she took his advice, for a few hours later he phoned from the hospital to Edith's flat and asked her to break the news to Nicola that her aunt had died from the stroke that had struck her down, without regaining consciousness, and that he was seeing to everything. When Edith passed on his message as gently as she knew how, Nicola took the news bravely. She grieved for her aunt, of course, for a few moments' insight into a sick woman's mind could not wipe out the regard she had felt for years, and she consoled herself by thinking that there must have been times in the past when Sarah had loved her a little, for love never begets hate, and she had loved her aunt dearly.

Dulcie, when informed of her mother's death, flatly refused to leave London to return to Carswell for the funeral. She quite brazenly stated that as her mother was dead she couldn't help her in any way, so she was staying put. Her utter heartlessness turned Nicola's stomach, so much so that she informed Dulcie that she never wanted to see her again. Her only answer was a flippant 'Suits me' before the telephone receiver was banged down and the line went dead. She was at least gracious enough to send a large floral tribute in memory of her mother, but the cold impersonality of the waxen flowers did not compensate Nicola for her absence from the funeral. She left the cemetery where Sarah was laid to rest for the last time with a terrible feeling of desolation that came from the knowledge that she was now completely alone in the world, with no one to care if she disappeared into Limbo.

That that feeling was unjustified, she was to find out in the following days, for her friends rallied round her with comforting regard. Edith insisted that she stay on in the flat as long as she wished, and as she had no desire to live alone in her aunt's house, she gladly accepted the invitation to use the flat as a base while she sorted out Sarah's belongings and got rid of her furniture, prior to leaving for London. Liz, too, sent constant reminders that she was thinking of her and longing to have her back —Dulcie having left without so much as a goodbye— while Charles Devlin had been a pillar of strength to her during the trying time that had had to be lived through.

She tried not to think of Matt. She had not set eyes on him since the day in the office when they had had the dreadful scene that had culminated in her confrontation with her aunt and its terrible consequences. He had sent flowers and a short note of sympathy, but had not once ventured near her, nor even sent a message with Charles, who had been a constant visitor to the flat in the past week. She was due to leave Carswell for ever in two days' time, and she had resigned herself to the idea of never seeing him again. The hurt of it was far worse than any she had borne since her aunt's death, and was responsible, more than any other factor, for the wave of desolation that shook her as she sat on the window-seat of the now empty drawing-room watching the surging fury of the waterfall in full spate as it impelled its pent-up energy into the bay below.

Everything was finished. The furniture was gone and only the ghosts of her childhood were left to remind her of the days she had spent growing from child to woman under the shelter of the roof that would shortly house some other family. She could hardly believe she would never again run up the short drive to the front door or sit where she was at that moment, watching the waterfall and the backcloth of her beloved fells. Even Rufus had had to have another home found for him and was to join a family of youngsters with whom he was friendly and where he would be perfectly content. She looked down at him as he lay at her feet, his head on his paws, waiting for a hoped-for walk. Even as she watched, he gave a low deep-throated growl and his ears pricked up as instinct told him they were no longer alone. She looked towards the door and saw Charles Devlin watching her with grave concern.

'I thought I might find you here, Nicola. Brooding?'

'No,' she answered, glancing round, 'just saying a last goodbye.'

'You're quite determined to leave us, then?'

The shadow that clouded her face did not escape his notice, nor did the sad inflection in her voice when she told him, 'There's nothing to keep me in Carswell now.'

'Nicola, my dear,' Charles sounded distressed, 'there will always be a place for you here. I should be the happiest of men if you would come to stay with us, and I don't mean just for a visit, I mean to live with us at Blaise House, permanently. You know how much I loved your mother, my dear. I lost her, but it would be like having a bit of her near me always, if you would only agree to my suggestion. Won't you think about it, Nicola? Please.'

Hysterical laughter rose to Nicola's throat at the very idea. To live at Blaise House with Charles! To meet Matt at every turning, sit with him for every meal! The mere idea of it was torture and she could hardly keep the panic out of her voice as she answered:

'Oh, no! I'm sorry, Charles, but it's out of the question!' She checked her outburst when she saw the light go out of his eyes, to be replaced by a small flicker of hurt that made her feel ashamed. Her voice softened, and she put her hand on his in an effort to make him understand that it was not *his* company she objected to.

'It wouldn't work, Charles,' she told him firmly. 'You've forgiven me for the things I said, but Matt never will. I must leave Carswell, but I'll never forget you, or your kindness. Mere words couldn't express my gratitude for all you've done for me.' She stood on tiptoe and placed a light kiss on his cheek. 'Thank you, Charles, with all my heart.'

He was deeply moved, and when, after a few seconds, he managed to speak, his voice was gruff with emotion.

'It's I who should thank you, my dear, for bringing a little light into an old man's life. If you're determined to go, then there's nothing else for me to say, except that I would like your promise that you'll keep in touch. I don't intend to allow you to slip out of my life altogether. Besides,' sadness settled over his face and was strangely at variance with the deliberate heartiness he forced into his voice, 'I want to know the date of your wedding, because of course I shall be sending you a present, my dear.'

Nicola flushed a brilliant scarlet and quickly protested, 'Oh, no, you mustn't . . . !'

At Charles's puzzled look, she added lamely :

'I don't expect I'll be getting married for ages yet. I haven't even considered setting a date or anything . . .' Her voice trailed away in miserable silence. Charles was taken aback.

'But I thought from what Matt said that the wedding was to be soon. Has he misunderstood you, perhaps?'

Nicola felt dreadful. She hated deceit, and still more she hated deceiving Charles. For the past few weeks he had been a tower of strength. His arm had been the one she had leaned upon during the dreadful time that had had to be lived through, and now, with his steady eyes upon her, she felt it impossible to be less than truthful with him. Baldly, for she could think of no way of dressing up the deed, she told him :

'I lied to Matt. I'm not marrying Jimmy, now, or any other time !'

She was staring past his head, or she would have seen the quick look of relief that transformed his face. He quickly resumed his grave expression, however, and managed to keep the joy he was feeling under control when he answered.

'Hrmmph . . . Well, my dear, it's none of my business, and I suppose you had a good reason for what you did, but I'm pleased you told me . . . very pleased.'

She turned away sharply and made towards the door with the ever-vigilant Rufus at her heels.

'Where are you going?' Charles queried sharply.

She didn't turn her head when she answered him lest he should notice the distress she felt sure was written on her face.

'I'm taking Rufus for a last walk,' she threw over her shoulder. 'Will you lock up here?'

To her surprise, he didn't demur, but answered, 'Yes, child, I'll see to everything, don't worry.'

He stood at the window and watched her slight figure

until she was almost out of sight, then, with a smile of satisfaction, he moved swiftly to the telephone and asked to speak to Matt.

The first impetus of Nicola's flight gradually slowed down to a desultory amble. She wandered along, drinking in her favourite sights to store them away in her mind's eye to be brought out and relished when, back in London, the only things to be seen outside her office window would be the bare bricks and expanse of plate-glass windows of the offices opposite. She registered to herself as she passed each one—that'll be the last time I shall see the cuddly brown and white calves fighting playfully amongst themselves in the field on the opposite side of the river—the last time I'll wander through this meadow and gaze at the fells in the far distance—the last time I'll watch the incredible grace of the swans as they glide in and out of the willows. She derided herself as a nostalgic idiot, but when she saw in the distance the hut where she had first met Matt she knew she simply had to take another last look, even though the sight would be bound to bring more pain than pleasure.

She turned off the track and made her way through the hillocks of grass up the incline to where the hut stood. She had come to the back of it, and slowly wandered round to the front, meaning to take a last peep inside before returning home. She turned the corner and stopped abruptly, her heart leaping, to see Matt leaning negligently against the hut as if waiting for someone. He looked devastatingly handsome, the light slacks and black polo-necked sweater he was wearing showing up his saturnine good looks to perfection. She gave an appalled gasp and swung round as if to take flight. As if expecting this reaction, Matt swiftly covered the space between them and planted himself firmly in front of her.

'Hello, Nicola,' he grinned, 'surprised to see me?'

She glared up at him, hating him for being so complacently sure of himself, and said just one word :

'You . . . !'

For once, her antagonism didn't seem to bother him, because he kept on smiling as he queried :

'Taking a last look round ?'

'Yes,' she answered briefly.

'Before you leave for London to get married ?'

This disconcerted her so much she found it impossible to answer. To her horror her eyes filled with quick tears and she tried to turn away before he saw them, but even as she took her first step she felt his arms on her shoulders pinning her to the spot. She couldn't bear him to touch her and began to struggle, ineffectually, against his superior strength, but when she found it impossible to budge she lifted her green eyes, swimming with tears, and pleaded with him brokenly :

'Please let me go. Haven't I provided you with enough amusement without this ?'

His answer was to pull her against his hard chest with a muttered imprecation and to ask her through gritted teeth :

'For the love of heaven, Nicola, what does a man have to do to make you believe that he loves you ? You know I can't keep my hands off you and I've been trying for weeks to get through to you, but you snub me every time. How can I convince you, Nicola ?'

She was so still and quiet, her head against his chest so that he couldn't see her face, that he was encouraged, diffidently, to go on. He tightened his arms around her and leaned his head until his lips were almost against her ear, and whispered :

'I love you, Nicola, my darling. I've loved you since I first met you on this very spot all those weeks ago. Will you put me out of my misery and tell me, one way or another, if there's any chance that you might be able to return my love . . . enough for you to marry me?'

She lifted her head as his impassioned plea penetrated her numbed senses to look wonderingly at his anxious face. She wanted desperately to believe him, but with the memory of a hurt still fresh in her mind, she whispered low:

'But you said I was a . . . cheat. That as a woman . . .'

He broke in, 'And you said I spent most of my time chasing female employees !'

'Oh, but I didn't mean it . . . !'

He swiftly interrupted. 'No, my darling, and I didn't mean it either. We've spent most of our time hurting each other.'

The sudden wondrous joy that was beginning to dawn in her eyes was caught by his. With a groan of unendurable anguish he buried his face against the soft whiteness of her neck and begged her:

'Nicola, I want most desperately to kiss you. Please say you won't turn on me like a spitfire, as you've done on every other occasion, if I do?'

All Nicola managed to say was, 'Oh, Matt darling !' but it was enough. He took her trembling mouth and covered it with his own, kissing her so thoroughly that when he at last lifted his head to look into her eyes she was as weak and helpless as a kitten and had to cling to him for support.

Neither of them seemed capable of assimilating the wonder of the moment, and it was very much later when they managed to force their minds on to a much lower plane and were able to speak coherently.

She teased him, a delightful colour staining her cheeks as he kissed her once more with his eyes.

'You know, Matt, there was no other possible outcome but that I should marry you.'

He fell in with her teasing mood and asked her lazily :

'And why was there no other possible outcome?'

'Because,' she smiled at him deliciously, 'all the girls in the typing pool bet on me in the lottery, and with all those good wishes behind me I couldn't fail to win!'

His curiosity aroused, she had to tell him about the lottery and the part he had played in it. When she finished her explanation, he was helpless with laughter, and as they turned to go home they were still in a paroxysm of mirth as they neared the house where Charles had been anxiously waiting, uncertain whether he had done the right thing in betraying Nicola's confidence to Matt, and praying that his instinct had not been unfounded when it told him that they loved each other. He darted to the window as he heard their happy laughter, and when he saw them walking towards him, their arms entwined, their faces ablaze with happiness, he gave silent thanks that, even though he had been denied his happiness, he would be able to relive his youthful hopes and dreams and see them fulfilled through them.

Shadows filled the room and he felt a whisper of a happy sigh, as if someone leaned over his shoulder and watched the happy pair advance towards the house. Standing quite still, Charles spoke into the silent room.

'They'll live out our happiness for us, Marcia, my love. The happiness we should have found together.'

Then, smiling contentedly, Charles walked out to meet them.

TITLES STILL IN PRINT

TO OUR DEVOTED HARLEQUIN READERS
FOR INFORMATION ON FORTHCOMING NEVER-BEFORE-PUBLISHED
HARLEQUIN ROMANCE TITLES, WRITE TO:

HARLEQUIN ROMANCE BOOKS
DEPARTMENT Z
SIMON & SCHUSTER, INC.
11 WEST 39TH STREET
NEW YORK, N.Y. 10018